WHERE, OH WHERE, HAS MOSLEY GONE?

Miss Crane went into the other rooms calling Janie by name, but without response. In the meanwhile Miss Stirrup had gone into the kitchen, where she found what she believed to be a patch of blood, still slightly tacky, on the strip of coconut matting in front of the sink. She also found an empty quart Guinness bottle, whose label was stained with what seemed to be the same sticky substance. To this congealment there adhered a few wisps of grey hair.

Georgina Crane remained in admirable control. She forbade Elizabeth Stirrup to touch anything more. She drove them fast back to old Mr. Cromwell's cottage, where she had just seen Mosley mowing the lawn, hoping to enlist his expertise.

But Mosley was no longer there. . . .

Agatha Christie

Death on the Nile
A Holiday for Murder
The Mousetrap and Other Plays
The Mysterious Affair at Styles
Poirot Investigates
Postern of Fate
The Secret Adversary
The Seven Dials Mystery
Sleeping Murder

Patricia Wentworth

The Ivory Dagger
Miss Silver Comes to Stay
Poison in the Pen
She Came Back

Margery Allingham

Black Plumes
Dancers in Mourning
Deadly Duo
Death of a Ghost
The Fashion in Shrouds
Flowers for the Judge
Pearls Before Swine

Dorothy Simpson

Close Her Eyes
Last Seen Alive
The Night She Died
Puppet for a Corpse
Six Feet Under

John Greenwood

The Missing Mr. Mosley
Murder by Moonlight
Murder, Mr. Mosley

Catherine Aird

Harm's Way
Henrietta Who
His Burial Too
Last Respects
Parting Breath
Slight Mourning

Elizabeth Daly

The Book of the Lion
Unexpected Night

Anne Morice

Murder in Outline
Murder Post-Dated
Scared to Death
Sleep of Death

John Penn

An Ad for Murder
A Deadly Sickness
Mortal Term
Stag Dinner Death
A Will to Kill

Ruth Rendell

No More Dying Then
Shake Hands Forever
A Sleeping Life
A Dark-Adapted Eye (writing as
   Barbara Vine)

The Missing Mr. Mosley

John Greenwood

BANTAM BOOKS

TORONTO · NEW YORK · LONDON · SYDNEY · AUCKLAND

All the characters and events portrayed
in this story are fictitious.

This low-priced Bantam Book
has been completely reset in a type face
designed for easy reading, and was printed
from new plates. It contains the complete
text of the original hard-cover edition.
NOT ONE WORD HAS BEEN OMITTED.

THE MISSING MR. MOSLEY
A Bantam Book / published by arrangement with
Walker Publishing Company, Inc.

PRINTING HISTORY
Walker edition published in January 1986
Bantam edition / December 1986

Bantam Books are published by Bantam Books, Inc. Its trademark,
consisting of the words "Bantam Books" and the portrayal of
a rooster, is Registered in U.S. Patent and Trademark Office
and in other countries. Marca Registrada. Bantam Books, Inc.,
666 Fifth Avenue, New York, New York 10103.

PRINTED IN THE UNITED STATES OF AMERICA

KR   0 9 8 7 6 5 4 3 2 1

The
Missing
Mr.
Mosley

1

"It had better be looked into," the Assistant Chief Constable said. "The *Hemp Valley Advertiser*? Who's our man in the Hemp Valley?"

"Mosley," Detective-Superintendent Grimshaw said, with that look of reluctant apology that drained his features whenever he had to admit that responsibility. "And he's just started his annual leave."

The relationship between Grimshaw and Mosley was not entirely straightforward. More than once in the past, against all the canons of sane judgement, Grimshaw had found himself defending Mosley in indefensible positions. And Mosley was not beyond finding himself in an indefensible position, even on holiday. The ACC, on the other hand, had never taken any chances in his defence.

"Well, that's a good thing from everybody's point of view," he said. "You'd better slip up there and cast an eye over it yourself, Tom. Just to be on the safe side. Find out who owns this thing. Ask him what the hell he's been doing with it. And if he's had any answers to his advertisement, find out who's shown any interest. Try to fathom his motives. Just in case, Tom."

"Mosley could probably tell us," Grimshaw said. "He does have a habit of knowing what's going on in those parts."

"All the same, let's wallow in such luxuries as Providence affords. Let Mosley recharge whatever it is that's

1

doing relief duty for his batteries. Where has he gone
for his leave?"

"The Hemp Valley, I believe."

"Is he mad?"

The Assistant Chief Constable had more than once
provided a spontaneous answer to that question.

"I'm speaking figuratively, sir. What I mean is, he
usually does spend his leave dodging about in his own
area. But he always takes strong exception to being
treated as if he were available for duty."

"All the same, you could just find him and ask him—"

"I think I'll nip up and see for myself, sir."

He looked down again at the newspaper cutting that
the Chief had passed him.

> *FOR SALE:* GALLOWS. In good working order.
> £10 o.n.o.
> Box No 862. HVA.

Grimshaw looked in his diary, to see when he could
spare a couple of hours.

2

---

*From the diary of Elizabeh Stirrup for Thursday, 7
April*

Drove the last sixty miles in increasing anxiety.
Is there any wisdom in trying to revive the ambiguous past? Felt more comfortable within an hour of

arrival. Miss Crane (she wants me to call her Georgie!) has changed, but she is brisk and alert, despite ageing joints. And she has become astoundingly worldly. Or perhaps *worldly* is hardly the word to use. The *world* is different in the Hemp Valley.

Wild countryside—I had expected its reputation to be exaggerated. The landscape is untamed (untamable?) and the wind round the Old Schoolhouse last night was of the sort that taught primitive man to believe in evil gods.

Except for drystone walls, subsiding in places into their own rubble—many of them dated from the earliest Enclosure Acts—it was possible to take in whole quadrants of landscape unscarred by man: except for man's sheep, who wandered as they would have done if they had belonged to no one. And except for the Old Railway, so overgrown that one could barely guess where the tracks had lain. Georgina evidently had a soft spot for the railway. She slowed up on a crest—a *brow*, she called it, almost childishly proud of the way she had adopted local words—so that they could look at a gritstone bridge that carried a farmer's track over a cutting. Two parties of young people were strung out along the bank, one of them of schoolchildren in bobbed woollen caps, carrying haversacks. The other, smaller group was of older adolescents, carrying more portentous equipment: clipboards, a theodolite, measuring chains and surveyors' stakes.

"You see, it's all come and gone. The Industrial Revolution gashed its way even across this fell. But the fell has claimed its own back. Those youngsters are looking for traces of what their grandparents grew up with."

It was Friday noon. They were doing Meals on Wheels, had driven to a dye-works canteen in a grimy valley bottom, where the food was cooked, and were going the rounds of isolated old people in frighteningly remote hill cottages. How did anyone survive a winter up here?

There seemed to be a super-abundance of *characters*—
or was the Heron romanticizing as of old? A woman
called Emily Smithers had an arthritic hip and could
barely get across to the ancient side-oven in which she
was warming her plate. Yet Miss Crane said it would be
wrong to make any move to help her: she needed to
believe in her independence. And the old girl laughed
like a middle-school educationally subnormal over some
X-rated horror she said she had seen last night on the
telly.

At another home they stopped, not to deliver food,
but apparently just to pass the time of day. It was a
modern building, but in the local stone and with the
local lines: squat, defiant, uninformative about itself.
And it was swarming with children, snotty-nosed and
broken-kneed, sturdily unaware that they had just passed
through one of the harshest winters in Hemp Valley
memory. The sole responsible adult seemed to be a
dirty old crone in her advanced seventies, who was
even less mobile than the woman with the bad hip.

"Squatters," Georgina Crane said. "But respectable.
All the adults are out working—or looking for work.
The house was built for themselves by a married couple
who have never lived in it—who, in fact, have never
cohabited at all. That's a tale for tonight—"

"But are those children *safe*?"

"Perfectly—and *loved*. Grandma can cope. I look in
twice a week: Age Concern. Just to keep track. But we
don't like to interfere with any domestic set-up that is
obviously working."

They called at a cottage two hundred years old, the
prototype of the squatters' place: a dead garden, littered with the detritus of survival—abandoned cold-
frames, an upturned old copper boiler, rhubarb pushing
up through the holes with which it was riddled, a
museum-piece gas cooker, lying on its back.

"The Protectorate," it said over the door, in home-
painted lettering, unevenly spaced and inconsistently
styled.

"His name's Cromwell," Miss Crane said. "Given names John William, but known in our little world as Noll. A Roundhead, warts and all. He will do his best to be insulting. If he says anything gross, say something gross back at him. That's what he's angling for—stimulus."

From the back of the house came the sounds of a mower—a strenuous rhythm of short jolts and jerks, as if the blades were jammed, clogged, or worn beyond redemption. The worker was a short, stubby man in a black homburg hat and an unbuttoned raincoat that flapped shapelessly behind him as he pushed at a machine which refused to go more than a yard at a time without human attention to its cogs. Miss Crane gave him good morning. But the first reaper of the season, undaunted by the temperament of his machine, pushed stubbornly on with his back to them, deaf to her voice.

Indoors, the latterday Protector was sitting at his kitchen table, eating from a plate a rough-hewn wedge of bread, which he had plastered with soft yellow butter. He was another character in his seventies, and he was wearing an ancient felt hat.

"Did you forget we were coming today, Mr. Cromwell?"

"I was hoping you weren't," he said, extracting the maximum ill grace from the situation. "I thought the schools were on holiday, kitchens closed."

"They are. This has been cooked at the dye works."

"It looks like it. In the bloody dye. What's it supposed to be?"

"It's an excellent casserole."

"I shall try it on the bloody cat first."

"If you waste it, I shall see you get no more. Ever. And watch your language. I have a lady with me."

Cromwell gave Elizabeth Stirrup the advantage of a lewd rolling eyeball.

"Feed her up a bit. She could be good for a tumble in a hayrick if she had a bit of flesh on her bones."

"Don't be so disgusting. I see you have free labour outside."

"That interfering bugger!"

"You ought to be grateful. And why do you have to keep swearing? Can't you use some word like flipping? Why is Mr. Mosley mowing your lawn?"

"It's do-flipping-good week, for some flipping club he flipping belongs to. I told him, if he could get the flipping wheels to flipping turn, he was welcome to try to push the flipping thing."

"Self-educated," Georgina said, as they let themselves out. "Quite remarkably well read—though unselectively, of course. A married man. I was best man at his wedding."

She was hardly recognizable as the Miss G. Crane, BA (Hons), who had fired E. Stirrup with enthusiasm for Keats and Jane Austen in the Lower Sixth.

"Best man at his wedding," Elizabeth said. "That's not a bad throwaway line."

"Somebody had to make sure he knew where to look for the altar."

"And where's his wife?"

"We shall be calling on her next. They are the couple I told you had never lived together."

"You mean the ones who built the house that the squatters are in?"

"Correct. He had been courting Janie Goodwin for eighteen years."

"What went wrong?"

"More than one thing. And there's more than one theory. Almost everyone in Hempshaw End has a separate version. Good morning, Mr. Mosley. You didn't hear me when I spoke to you just now."

The mower was manhandling his contraption for a return trip across the prairie, and was now facing them. He waved with what might have been merriment, except that his face wore the expression of concentrated ferocity that the rusty machinery demanded of him. He was a man in his fifties, fell-weathered, and with something hobgoblinish in the tilt of his eyebrows. He stooped to ease back the cutting-cylinder and removed a large chunk of badly bruised grass.

"He's a Detective-Inspector," Georgina whispered. "We don't see a lot of him. They never seem to provide him with proper transport, so he has to walk the fells from one crime to another. Not that Hempshaw End has contributed to the Chamber of Horrors."

They got into her car and skirted the village. Hempshaw End had rather fewer than a thousand inhabitants, settled about the spider's legs of three cloughs and the brook-valley that they fed. There were elderly couples here who remembered having to live off what the soil had to offer. Nowadays most people commuted to Bradburn, where they made some sort of livelihood out of selling things to each other. There were one or two who, in pursuit of some far-fetched dream, had come here to retire. Janie Goodwin lived in a small and expressionless cottage at the lower end, set in a stony triangular patch, which she had trimmed into a well-informed rock garden.

Georgina pulled in close under Janie's wall. Why, Elizabeth wondered, was she still called Goodwin if she was married to Cromwell? Presumably Hempshaw End was either immovably conservative or bluntly realistic.

Georgina went to the boot to get Janie Goodwin's stew and supporting stodge. Elizabeth waited for her by Janie's gate, looking idly at her rather natty lace curtains, oddly at odds with the card bearing the roughly sketched outline of a fish, which stood on the upper ledge of the window: a rudimentary design, with a V mouth, a round eye and deformed fins—incongruous against the generally well-cared-for window-space. There were luxuriant growths of epiphyllum, potted hyacinths and a wealth of pedestalled greenery. Georgina, when she reappeared, was curiously startled by the sight of the diagrammatic fish.

"She refused to participate. She was bitter and blasphemous when we spoke to her about it."

There was no time for an explanation now. Georgina

eventually told Elizabeth the facts. The fish sign—the younger woman had a feeling of mild guilt that she ought to have known—had apparently been widely used as a call for recognition and succour among the early Christian churches and it had been adopted as a cry for help by one of the twentieth-century organizations with which Georgina busied herself. In case of emergency, old people were implored to put their fish sign in their windows. Janie Goodwin, whatever her crisis, had evidently had to sketch her own. She was a woman as scornful of society in her own way as her husband, John William Cromwell, was in his. There were certain strata with which she did not care to be identified, and she apparently found little to admire in professed Christians.

So if she was appealing to them now . . .

It looked, when they opened the door, as if they were already too late to be of effective assistance. Janie Goodwin's living-room had been hurriedly and furiously wrecked. Pedestals had been knocked about the floor. A Wedgwood urn was in fragments, vases had been shattered, upholstery ripped and a sofa and two armchairs were lying on their backs. The first impression was that somewhere under all this destruction, Janie Goodwin must be helplessly pinned, and the women's first action was to manhandle broken furniture to see if they could find her. But there was no sign of the owner of the wreckage.

Miss Crane went into the other rooms calling Janie by name, but without response. In the meanwhile Miss Stirrup had gone into the kitchen, where she found what she believed to be a patch of blood, still slightly tacky, on the strip of coconut matting in front of the sink. She also found an empty quart Guinness bottle of obsolete pattern, whose label was stained with what seemed to be the same sticky substance. To this congealment there adhered a few wisps of grey hair.

Georgina Crane remained in admirable control. She forbade Elizabeth Stirrup to touch anything more than they had already touched. She drove them fast back to the Protectorate, hoping to enlist Mosley's expertise.

But Mosley was no longer there. Giving the decrepit old mower his best, he had apparently gone off to do unspecified good elsewhere.

3

"Does anyone know where I can find Mosley?"

And a delighted chorus informed Grimshaw of what he already knew.

"He's on leave, sir."

"But doesn't anyone know where he *is*?"

It was well known that Mosley never travelled far on his holidays. As often as not, an overdue bout of interior decoration in his own home brought him back to duty refreshed after only a few days.

"Put out discreet enquiries, someone."

It was not that Grimshaw felt that he needed Mosley. Indeed, he was tempted to agree with the ACC that Mosley's absence from a major enquiry was more than they had the right to hope for. But Hempshaw End was exclusively and peculiarly Mosley country. And—though not much of it had to do with crime—Mosley had a habit of knowing a good deal of what went on in his country. Moreover, Grimshaw had not yet had the time to trace the gentleman who had no further use for his gallows. And Mosley was bound to know.

But you could never be certain how Mosley might react to an attempt to interrupt his leave. He might

resent being omitted from debates about people whom
he regarded in some obscure sub-tribal way as belong-
ing to him. He did not exactly comport himself as a
minor chieftain, but there was more than a hint of the
witch-doctor about him. He did not like other people
trying to mix medicine on his patch—but on the other
hand he might vehemently refuse to be dislodged from
his repose.

But the Assistant Chief Constable was surprised that
Grimshaw should even momentarily want Mosley out
on the ground.

"Unless of course you have some private reason for
wanting the case to be strung out over a year or so."

"It's not that. I scent an eccentric."

"That's like 'The Leith Police dismisseth us.' We
ought to remember that one, in case they ever revive
the old type of drunken-driving test."

"What I mean, sir, is that Mosley does have his
friends."

"There is no accounting for people's tastes in people."

The on-the-spot evidence was not at all helpful. Like
everyone else in Hempshaw End, Janie Goodwin lived
with her back door unlocked. She put it on the chain
only when she went to bed. People in Hempshaw End
were not thieves. So there had been no difficulty of
access.

There were fingerprints about the room, but in the
absence of Janie, there was no way of establishing which
of these were her own. There were also the prints of at
least two other persons—presumably the Meals on
Wheels ladies. The blood from the kitchen matting and
the Guinness bottle was duly dispatched to Forensic.
There was not enough evidence to presume Janie dead,
but the prognosis did not look good. Of Janie herself,
alive or dead, there was no sign.

The road in which she lived was as busy as any
thoroughfare in Hempshaw End. It was sometimes said
that if someone in Top Lane turned the page of his
Hemp Valley Advertiser prematurely, there would be a

complaint in Hempshaw Bottoms from someone who had not finished reading the Births, Marriages and Deaths. But nobody that Grimshaw had spoken to—and he had gone out of his way to speak to a good many—had seen anything of Janie Goodwin that morning. Nor had they seen anyone go to her house. No one had seen her put the fish card up in her window. No one had observed it after it had been put there. Yet in every other respect this appeared to have been a normal weekday morning, and the residents of Hempshaw End, particularly the women, must surely have spent a proportion of their time padding about from one back door to another, passing on such items of non-news as had come to their attention.

And Grimshaw could not escape the galling certainty that if it had been Mosley asking the questions, the answers would have been more fruitful and less hesitant. Mosley would probably not have had to ask questions at all. People would have crossed busy roads to put him in the picture; that is, in the unlikely event that he was not, in his asinine way, in the picture already. It was remarkable in what a short space of time the absentee Mosley's reputation expanded in his Detective-Superintendent's mind. There were things about the natives of these back-hills that Mosley seemed to have known since the beginnings of time. Grimshaw, on the other hand, made no claim to having a way with rustic morons.

He thought he might do rather better with the two ladies who had discovered the chaos in the cottage. He went over to the former village primary school, a building almost a hundred and fifty years old, which Miss Crane had had converted to her own design. Grimshaw judged her to be in her early sixties: clearly a woman accustomed to say "Go!" whereupon people went. She was obviously intolerant of anything which did not seem to her to make sense; but the standard by which she judged what was sense was a personal one, to which she saw no reason to append footnotes.

Her companion was younger, probably by twenty
years or more. She was a woman who might possibly
have made herself look attractive if she had had any
leanings in that direction. It was not basically that she
neglected herself. Her skin was well cared for, her
cosmetics unadventurous but not inappropriate, her hair
very frequently shampooed. But her ambition seemed
to be solely not to offend. She would have hated to
excite anyone. And she said very little during the interview, except to confirm what her hostess said. She was
in all respects the uninvolved guest who had simply
happened in on all this.

Both women were subdued in the aftermath of their
experience. They wanted to be helpful in any way they
could, but could not really see ways of doing so.

"This Goodwin lady, and her husband, Miss Crane. I
keep being told stories of an unconsummated marriage.
I am having some difficulty in arriving at the facts."

"That does not surprise me. A good deal of imagination has been whetted on the subject. I fear you would
not find it relevant to your enquiry."

"At the present stage, I prefer to treat everything as
relevant."

"There seems to have arisen an acrimonious quarrel
on their way from the church to the reception. But this
was only a reflection of what had been going on throughout their eighteen-year courtship. As a result, they
never moved into the house they had built. It has now
been taken over by an underground association that
finds shelter for the homeless."

"And what have Mr. and Mrs. Cromwell had to say
about this trespass?"

"Nothing, to my knowledge. They are unselfish people. I would imagine they are both content to feel that
the place is doing someone some good."

"They are capable of agreeing about something, then?"

"Oh, yes. They have remained, after a fashion, very
good friends. It is only when they are together that
they fall out. Perhaps, Superintendent, you have some

difficulty in adjusting your mind to the little things that
loom large in a community such as ours? When one has
lived among these people, one becomes accustomed to
the things that go on."

"Perhaps. So are you in a position to tell me *what* is
going on?"

"Let us hope that it *is* 'is' and not 'was,' " Miss Crane
pleaded patiently. "Though I must say that the hairs on
that bottle looked to me remarkably like Janie Goodwin's. The point is, the Cromwells agreed to remain
apart. I expect they felt that that would make for a
quieter life. Though actually they do—did—oh, for goodness' sake let's say *do*—meet three times a week, on
Tuesdays, Fridays and Sundays at morning-coffee time.
Not that it is coffee they drink, one is given to understand. One gathers that both of them have redder-
blooded tastes than that."

Grimshaw had not risen in rank without a certain
mental acuity. He did recognize that today was Friday.
So this man Cromwell and the woman who had disappeared might well have been together at the time when
the woman's household effects were being destroyed.

But Miss Crane was still talking. "I cannot say whether
they met this morning, because I did not spend this
morning with them. Nor am I privy these days to the
confidences of either of them. It is true that I was best
man at their wedding, but since the rift in their lute,
neither of them has been to me for advice. I do know
that Cromwell was at his table by dinner time, because
I took him his dinner. But if you want more information
as to how he spent his morning, you had better ask
your friend."

"Friend? What friend?"

"Mr. Mosley."

"What has Mosley to do with it?"

"Mr. Mosley spent the morning mowing Mr. Cromwell's lawn."

Grimshaw did his best to maintain the serenity of his
features, to control the pitch of his voice and to manage

the evenness of his respiration. There was a surrealism about this case that was beginning to affect him like sea-sickness.

"You saw Mosley this morning?"

"I did."

"And where is he now?"

"I don't know. He simply seems to have gone away. I did not want to waste too much time looking for him."

Somehow, Mosley's disappearance at the crucial moment seemed predictable.

"This rift in the Goodwin–Cromwell lute: what was the immediate cause of it?"

"Different people have different ideas," Miss Crane said, and seemed to be having difficulty in fighting a wry smile away from her lips. "I doubt whether you would find it rewarding to explore them at this stage."

"At this stage I need to explore everything that there is to be explored."

The younger woman was looking on with silent neutrality.

"It is said that Janie was not prepared to tolerate the knots in Cromwell's bootlaces. There is one every half-inch or so. They are not very elegant."

Grimshaw was now looking at her with an expression of solemn patience, very consciously assumed.

"Actually, he can dress quite well, when occasion demands it. And in his earlier way of life, he had to pay more than lip-service to formality. But even at the most demanding of functions, he never made any attempt to do anything about his bootlaces. He even turned up at the altar in them. Mind you, I am not saying that that was all there was to it."

"I dare say not."

"I do know that for some years before the wedding she tried hard to get him to thread them crosswise. But he preferred them straight across, parallel from eyelet to eyelet. I think he probably considers that more masculine. Isn't *macho* a word much used nowadays?"

Grimshaw was not taking notes.

"Of course, if you ask in the village, you are likely to hear more sensational explanations. Some may tell you that they finally parted because she had insisted on wearing to her wedding a plastic raincoat, which squeaked when she walked, thus setting his teeth on edge. To my mind, bootlaces and plastic raincoats were only the superficial symptoms of a deeper-lying incompatibility."

When she spoke *ex cathedra*, Miss Crane had a voice that could have trooped a colour, and *ex cathedra* was the tone she considered fitting for a Detective-Superintendent.

"So you see the boot is not entirely on one foot. Oh, I'm sorry, I shouldn't have brought boots and feet up again. I'd hate you to think I'm trying to be facetious about it. But I must say that in my view they should never have married."

"Yet you seem to have taken an active part in promoting their union."

"Only to oblige, Mr. Grimshaw. Not that I'm claiming *noblesse*, you understand. As the Prayer Book has it, a ritual contract is preferable to fornication. For which policy of prudence we thank the ever-vigilant St. Paul, of course."

Grimshaw was saved from a Pauline digression by Miss Crane's doorbell. It was Sergeant Beamish, reporting for duty.

Beamish was the go-getting CID Sergeant from Q Division, an ambitious, intolerant and alarmingly energetic young man, whose up-to-dateness in his calling caused many senior officers to have to hold their peace in his presence. Grimshaw had had Beamish seconded to himself at Hempshaw End, and in so doing had applied a measure of casuistry. It was, he told himself, not merely in the hope of getting the case broken for him in double-quick time. There was also a certain sense of penance in wishing the young man's company upon himself. Other officers had had to put up with him. Beamish, according to reports, was not merely astringent. When working alongside the old guard, he could be nothing less than petrifying.

And there was another thing about Beamish. He had once worked on a case as Mosley's right-hand man, and it had been felt in high places at the time that within forty-eight hours of their introduction to each other, one or both of them would have retired from the force. On the contrary, for some reason not amenable to the ordinary processes of logic, they had taken to each other. The dilapidated Inspector and the forward-looking Sergeant might seem irreconcilably polarized, but when they had eventually returned to their separate duties, each was heard to crush casual public criticism of the other. Their cross-pollination had produced a subtle change of outlook on both sides. The hope flickered in Grimshaw's breast (may God and the ACC forgive him!) that something of Mosley's approach to bucolic lunatics might have rubbed off on Beamish. And that Beamish might have learned from his improbable idol how to cajole information from men whose brains were like the wool of moorland sheep, and whose words were about as substantial as wind-borne thistle-down.

Now Beamish stood in Miss Crane's doorway and awaited his superior's orders with an eye that obviously expected any instruction from above to be infantile and supererogatory. Perhaps, Grimshaw reflected with an effort at charity, Beamish was not to be judged by his face; mabe it had just been his misfortune to have been born with that look on it. It would do Beamish good to be kept waiting a minute or two; there was another matter still to be cleared up with Miss Crane.

"Do you," Grimshaw asked her, "know of anyone locally who has a gallows for sale?"

"Oh, dear—is, is it likely to come to that, Superintendent? But surely you don't expect to have to be your own executioner, do you? Capital punishment—"

"I can see that you have no information on the subject, Miss Crane." Grimshaw spoke to her a good deal more sharply than he had intended.

"I am sorry to disappoint you, Superintendent."

She looked at Elizabeth Stirrup as if her confidence in senior twentieth-century policemen was now perhaps within measuring distance of the ebb.

Grimshaw turned to what he now saw as distinctly safer ground. "Ah! Beamish!" He felt an absurd temptation to quote from *Jabberwocky*. "I left the scenes-of crime people, doing their scenes-of-crime stuff down at the scene-of-crime," Grimshaw said, but his burst of brightness was wasted on the impassive Beamish.

"Nip down there and see if they've turned up anything of interest."

"I called in on the way up, sir. I thought it would save time."

"Yes. Well?"

Beamish looked steadily at Grimshaw and let his eyelids flicker fractionally to remind him that two outsiders were present. Did an experienced officer really propose to discuss casework in front of people who might turn out to be accessories? How did men get to be made Superintendent?

"Shall we take a little walk, Sergeant?"

Grimshaw took his leave of the ladies and suggested that he might be back later for further enlightenment. Outside, he waited for further news of the day from Beamish. Beamish produced a bulldog-style briar pipe, protected from defilement in a small plastic bag.

"Found in the flowerbed under Mrs. Cromwell's front window, sir."

Trust Beamish to be scrupulous about the surname.

"It has obviously not been there overnight, sir. No dew or damp has penetrated to the ash. I would say that it has obviously been smoked this morning. The tar along the edge of the bowl is still slightly viscous to the touch."

"Yes—I had noticed that."

"I would say that it belongs to a man with a lower

denture, but who still has his own teeth in the upper jaw. Only a genuine canine could have produced that indentation."

"Clearly."

"A right-handed smoker. See the charring of the rim at this point, due to the repeated application of a lighted match."

"Very neat observation, Sergeant."

"And it was last smoked coming down this hill, I think. The wind today is from the south-east, and you can see where the most recent encrustation of the bowl has occurred."

"I was hoping you'd not fail to spot that, Sergeant."

"Cromwell's pipe, do you think, sir? I learn that he normally calls on his wife on Friday mornings. You will have gathered already, sir, that the pair are married——?"

"Yes, Sergeant. I am well aware of that. But if——"

"The marriage seems to have broken down within minutes of the ceremony, sir. One reason suggested for this is that Mrs. Cromwell took offence because he presented himself in the front pew wearing a medal on his watch-chain that he had won with a racing pigeon. She felt that that betrayed his true sense of values. Or words to that effect."

"Really?"

"I think there may have been some element of the last straw about it," Beamish said.

"Not improbably. What I was going to——"

"Another version is that she refused to live with him until he had been to a chiropodist. She told him that she was not prepared to spend the rest of her life looking at the nails on his big toes. One was like a lamb's ear, she said, and the other reminded her of a cockatoo's beak."

"Had she somehow caught sight of his big toe in church, then, Beamish?"

"No, sir, but she is said to have asked him in a whisper at some appropriate point in the service whether he had kept the appointment she had made for him."

"Beamish—"

"But you see, sir, he had apparently insisted that she have something done about her sinuses. It would seem that she snored. May I ask you a question, sir?"

"I will do my best, Beamish."

"Sir—what was all that about a gallows for sale?"

"You don't know about the gallows, Beamish?"

"No, sir."

"You haven't so far found time to read the case-notes?"

Grimshaw's tone was acid, but he was quick to remind himself that he was rarely as unfair to his sergeants as this. He relented and brought Beamish up to date.

"It's a pity that Inspector Mosley is on leave, sir. I dare say he knows all about that gallows. Do you think, sir, that for something as big as this, he would have any objection to being recalled from leave?"

"A bad principle," Grimshaw said. "Are you suggest-ing that we cannot handle this ourselves?"

"Not at all, sir. It is simply that Mosley has a way of talking to people."

"So have we, Beamish. Let's go and start on this Roundhead."

Noll Cromwell was asleep at the moment that they knocked on his door. Whatever he had felt about his wife's sinuses, his own snores penetrated a good three inches of oak. Grimshaw knocked and entered, and at very first sight it was obvious that Janie Goodwin had exercised no ultimate influence on those bootlaces. He had loosened them for sleep, and the tongues lolled out as if they belonged to some animal that had perished unstoically in a desert.

Cromwell opened one eye and inspected his visitors with a ripe distillate of misanthropy. It was an instant of unmitigated ill will—but an instant was all that it was. As Cromwell became fully awake, he registered a sar-donic amusement at the sight of them. If there was anything of which Noll Cromwell was certain, it was that he was a fair match for anyone who came at him

with mere words. He would enjoy casting them down.
He wished that more callers would come to take him
on. He leaned down and gave a single tug at each of the
notorious laces; and some reason for his obstinate reten-
tion of them now gained credibility. They were a work
of art. The spacing of his knots was such that one single
deft movement tightened everything within sight. Cromwell unbent himself with a wheezing aftermath of
respiratory distress.

"Do I take it that this is a professional call, gentlemen?"

"Indeed it is," Grimshaw said, assuming that he knew
who they were.

"Folks haven't told you that I've retired, then? I
don't dispose of people any more."

His eyes challenged argument.

"Leastways, I have half a dozen more to put away—as
personal favours. If you want their names—"

"We are not here to make crude jokes," the Detective-Superintendent said.

"I'd be sorry to offend you."

Cromwell looked sincerely concerned.

"But I always say that it's a mistake to take death too
seriously. I like to see people off with a bit of a smile,
you know. They're supposed to be on their way to
everlasting happiness, aren't they? So why bloody well
cry about it? Do we begrudge them their reward?"

"I think I should warn you, Mr. Cromwell—"

"Warn me, is it? Nobody's put in a complaint, have
they? Let me tell you, I've never had repercussions
from a customer yet. When I see them off, they stay
seen off. When I lay a man in his grave, he stays in it.
All bar one, and that was a special case—and he didn't
show up again, the second time I put him down. I don't
know what sort of reputation you think I've got—but
there's no call to come *warning* me. My Janie, Jed
Pearson, Billy Tucker, Stan Lomas, Harry Lamplough,
Dick Berry—when that lot have joined the Great Chorus, my work's finished. Now they tell me that John
Nall, over at Hadley Dale, does a tidy and respectful

job. And it stands to sense; he's learning all the time.
I've already exchanged contracts with him, for when my
big moment comes."

"What are you under the impression that we are
talking about?" Grimshaw asked him.

"Well, I've always thought it a silly word, but they
call me an undertaker. I used to be a builder, you
know, but I found myself specializing more and more.
So what is an undertaker? It's a man who undertakes to
do something, isn't it? It could go for gelding a tom cat
or icing a cake. You undertake to do it—you do it. I
undertake the ritual dispatch of mortal shells. But except for the six good friends already mentioned—"

"We are policemen, Mr. Cromwell—"

"Policemen? I thought that that daft bugger Mosley
was our guardian of the peace."

"I am Inspector Mosley's superior officer: Detective-
Superintendent Grimshaw. And I am sorry to have to
come upsetting you at the present time. But I must ask
you: how did you spend this morning?"

"Spend the morning? How do I spend any of my
mornings? Doing my housework."

Grimshaw was practised at sizing up rooms as an
indication of character, of way of life, of aspirations,
social and personal, but it could be easy to make mistakes about this one. There was so much in it—such a
welter of possessions—that dust was something that
Cromwell must long ago have decided that he had to
put up with. And it was not possible to tell how many of
these things were true treasures, how many of them
had simply arrived and not seemed worth the labour of
shifting. They might even be a façade maintained to
impress their owner's world. He had the works of Dick-
ens in a cheap uniform edition produced for newspaper
promotion in the 1930s. He had books on all manner of
things, from veterinary surgery to prosthetic dentistry—
books on theology, history and oriental travels. He had
Scott and Hardy, the *Meditations* of Marcus Aurelius
alongside Todhunter's *Trigonometry* and Gene Strat-

ton Porter. He had an early acoustic gramophone and a
stack of twelve-inch 78s, still in their tatty original
covers: Gilbert and Sullivan, *Les Cloches de Corneville*,
Puccini and Brahms. His morning's chores had taken no
account of the dust that lay on these. But it was true
that housework was done here daily. His frying-pan
looked regularly scoured. His sink and draining-board
were left clean and empty at the end of his washing-up.
There were no remnants in his garbage pail.

"And it's Friday today, you know. You wouldn't expect me to miss the schools programme on BBC. 'Threatened Species'!"

"At what time did you go down to the village to see
your wife?"

"I didn't, this morning."

"But it's Friday."

"I had a visitor."

"A visitor? All morning?"

Grimshaw had not forgotten, of course. But he waited
to be told.

"Jack Mosley. The daft bugger."

"He's a friend of yours, is he?"

"We've known each other for years."

"Mr. Cromwell, I want you to be careful how you
answer this—I happen to know that Inspector Mosley is
on leave this week—"

"So he told me. That's why he came to mow my
lawn. I didn't ask him to. I didn't want him to. I told
him the mower was no bloody good. He found that out
for himself in due course."

"So what was all this in aid of?"

"He belongs to some club that goes about interfering
with the privacy of senior citizens—like digging their
plots, papering their rooms, chopping their kindling."

"And mowing your lawn?"

"To the best of his ability—with a machine that's
stood out all the winter. He had to call it master."

"How long was he here?"

"I don't know. I wasn't keeping a time-sheet on him."

"And you were here all the time he was?"

"You don't think I'd leave a copper alone on the premises, do you?"

"Where did he go from here?"

"He didn't say. I didn't even know he'd left."

Sergeant Beamish had managed to withdraw from Cromwell's immediate arc of vision and was moving unobtrusively about the room. He looked at a letter which had been opened and folded back into its envelope. He looked at an air-rifle leaning in a corner, at a framed photograph of a woman.

Cromwell must suddenly have sensed his progress. He hoisted himself abruptly from his chair and bellowed: "If it's a conducted tour you want, I'll be happy to oblige. But unless you tell me what you have on your minds, gentlemen . . ."

Grimshaw made no effort to placate him. He got up and went round to the portrait that Beamish had been examining. It was a glossy enlargement from a fixed-focus snapshot. The camera had not been held straight, so the drably dressed woman caught shopping in a High Street seemed to be listing at a perilous angle. She was scowling at the unwelcome photographer.

"When did you last see your wife, Mr. Cromwell?"

"When did I last see her? Tuesday, I suppose. We generally sip a tot of rum together on a Tuesday."

"And Fridays, as a rule, don't you? Today's Friday, Mr. Cromwell."

"I've already told you—Jack Mosley came, and he started mowing, then I brewed tea, and he came in and sat through the schools broadcast with me."

"And talked to you?"

"Of course he bloody well talked to me."

"About your wife?"

"You seem very interested in my wife, Superintendent."

It was impossible to tell to what extent Cromwell was acting this naïveté.

"Was this a friendly visit, Mr. Cromwell—or had Mosley something on his mind?"

"Who's ever to tell what Jack Mosley has on his mind? I've heard it said, when he's at his most friendly, that's the time to put your shutters up."

"So he had you worried, had he?"

And Cromwell laughed—with a violence that looked as though it might get out of hand.

"Me? Worried by Jack Mosley? What am I supposed to have done?"

His innocence had an almost frightening ring to it. If this was an evil man, Grimshaw reflected, then it was a very hideous evil indeed.

"Is it true, Mr. Cromwell, that you and your wife have never lived together?"

"I dare say you'd like to know whether the marriage was ever consummated. That's the word they use, isn't it?"

Cromwell could use big words with facility. Perhaps he had read some of the books with which his room was stacked and littered. Grimshaw was beginning to feel out of his depth. It was a totally different type of question that Mosley would have been asking here and now. Nevertheless, Grimshaw threw himself bravely at the incisive question now. After all, it was Cromwell who had raised the subject.

"And *was* the marriage ever consummated?"

"Not after the ceremony," Cromwell said.

Period. Cromwell looked at Grimshaw, challenging him to follow that up. And Beamish was looking at Grimshaw as if pleading for a display of that kind of expertise that a sergeant has the right to be shown by the head of his department.

"The relationship between you and your wife defeats me," Grimshaw said.

"Admitting for the sake of argument that it is any of your business, it has so far defeated us, Superintendent."

"So why am I making it my business?" Grimshaw asked him.

"God knows."

"Cromwell—I am almost tempted to believe that you do not know what happened at your wife's cottage this morning."

Cromwell looked at him for some seconds as if this was something that officialdom considered clever. But he could not now miss seeing that the gravity behind Grimshaw's eyes was not faked.

"As true as God's my judge, I've not been out all day. What are you trying to tell me?"

"I'm sorry to have to be this kind of messenger."

Grimshaw described quietly and fully the scene that the two women had found. Cromwell accepted the facts without the bluster that Grimshaw had been more than half expecting. One might almost have thought that he was listening without emotion. But he could not speak at first when Grimshaw had finished.

And behind him, across the room, Beamish was trying to mouth a silent word to the Superintendent.

"I can assure you, Mr. Cromwell, that we as a force are what we call pulling the stops out. We are a big organization, and we shall spare nothing to get to the bottom of this. And it is far too early yet for you to give up hope. Sergeant Beamish—are you trying to communicate with me?"

"You have an exhibit, sir," Beamish prompted.

"An exhibit?"

"Placed carefully in a plastic envelope not much more than an hour ago, sir," Beamish said, splendidly cryptic—and too damned clever by half.

"Ah!"

Grimshaw produced the bulldog pipe, took it out of its wrapping and laid it down on the table in front of Cromwell.

"When did you last see this?"

"Earlier today."

"You did, did you? And may I ask when and where?"

"Jack Mosley was smoking it."

The pipe was of no interest to Cromwell. He leaned across the table and gripped Grimshaw's wrist. "Are you trying to tell me you think Janie's dead?"

"Let me see you hold this pipe between your teeth, Mr. Cromwell."

"Put it back in its little bag, Superintendent. And give it back to Mosley next time you see him. Didn't Sherlock Holmes once write a paper about tobacco ash? What was it he called it? A monograph? You'll find that bowl is choked with Mosley's filthy black Cavendish. I've smoked thin twist all my life; that's pure tobacco—nothing but tobacco. And now tell me about Janie."

"I can't tell you more about Janie than I've told you already. Until we find her—and we must pray that she has come to no harm—"

"I'm her next of kin, Mr. Grimshaw. I have my rights."

"Everyone has his rights. And everyone's rights will be respected. And if you want to help, you'll give me straight answers to just a few more straight questions."

"You can try asking. But I don't think I know more than you do, Superintendent."

"Had your wife any enemies?"

"What is an enemy?"

"Someone who'd smash up her home and beat her about the head with an empty bottle."

"Not that kind of enemy."

"So what kind of enemy had she?"

"A relief milkman who tried to make her pay for a pint she hadn't had. Nothing more savage than that. And that didn't lead to blows."

"What about the earlier part of her life?"

"That's something I can't tell you all that much about."

"Was she born and brought up in these parts?"

"You might say she was, and you might say she wasn't."

"That sort of answer isn't very helpful, Mr. Cromwell."

"But it's true. She was a Goodwin. That means she was born in Hempshaw End—but she never belonged."

"How come?"

"The Goodwins had the big house. At one time."

"And I suppose there are all sorts of slanderous stories connected with them?"

"You ought to ask Jack Mosley about that."

"Inspector Mosley isn't here. I'm asking you."

"I'm not a reliable witness. I'm too close to the matter."

"What matter?"

"The Goodwins. Go and ask Mosley."

"Mr. Cromwell, stop being evasive. I'm asking you to tell me anything vaguely connected with you and your wife, which might suggest why anyone should want to harm her. Don't try to decide what to tell me and what not to tell. Leave it to me to make up my mind what's useful and what isn't."

It was a bedrock obstinacy that had come over Cromwell. If he was a difficult man at the best of times, he could clearly be impossible when he had set his mind on some private course. He was beginning to feel the stress of what he had been told, and he was going to need long-term pressure. Grimshaw did not want to be drawn into a stultifying cross-talk act in front of Beamish.

"I shall be back to see you again, Mr. Cromwell. In the meanwhile, be getting things straight in your own mind. Start working out a plain and helpful statement. If you can't give me one in a few hours' time, I shall begin to think that there are things you don't want me to know about."

Cromwell looked at him with eyes that might possibly be pitying him for his wide-ranging ignorance of all the things that mattered in life.

"I must ask you to hold yourself at my disposal. There will be a lot of policemen about for the next twenty-four hours or so. If you are thinking of going out of the village, let them know of your intentions."

"And where do you think I'd be likely to go?" Cromwell asked him.

They walked some way away from the Protectorate before Grimshaw informed Beamish what he had in mind.

"We'll lay on a staggered relief of DCs and aides to keep an eye on Cromwell. We'll make the biggest box-search of the surrounding countryside that we can muster the manpower for. But we've only another hour or two before daylight begins to fade, and there's not much we can do in this kind of country in the dark, except stumble about. Beamish—you know Mosley pretty well—"

"I've worked with him."

"Successfully. That in itself is a news item. Have you worked with him in this area?"

"No, sir."

"So you won't know who his local contacts are. But you know what sort of people they'd be?"

Beamish permitted himself to show private amusement.

"Have I said something funny, Sergeant?"

"With respect, sir, I can't help seeing the humorous side. Mosley's likely contacts—"

"A richly varied lot, obviously."

"And not easy to detect. I use that word carefully."

"So your immediate task, Beamish, is to find Mosley."

Beamish came to attention—not with arms, legs and feet, but with eyes that spelled out his readiness to comply at once with the impossible.

"Tell him to report to me, leave or no leave."

"Sir."

4

From the diary of Elizabeth Stirrup for Friday, 8 April

A day unique for its alarums and excursions. And at the end of it, a quiet hour with Georgina. But not in communion with her—as I had paradoxically hoped and feared. It is difficult to believe that at the age of thirteen I had a crush on this woman, that in passionate daydreams I tried to persuade myself that she was not less aware of me. I thought in those days that she was the easiest of women to understand. Tonight I am confused.

Georgina was shaken. After they had finally taken the Meals on Wheels gear back to the dye works, neither of them fancied lunch. Elizabeth felt sick but could not be sick. Georgina disappeared into her bedroom, and when she came back, there was drink on her breath. She now poured Martinis Bianco for both of them. It was unthinkable that in her teaching days she had been anything but a strict teetotaller.

She talked about Janie Goodwin-Cromwell, about whose previous life there seemed to be as much of a mystery as about her marriage. She had been one of a number of daughters at Hempshaw Hall, the large house just beyond the lower end of the village—a residence that might have been thought of as a manor, had it not been so well known that Wilson Goodwin had mort-

29

gaged every brick, stone and slate of it. "The monkey on the chimney": that was the phrase that Hempshaw End had for it. The Goodwins had held themselves aloof from the village, Georgina said. Their interests, anyway, were not such as the village would have shared. Their music, their formalized horse-riding, their eating rituals, their house parties, were not on a plane that Hempshaw End saw much point in. What did delight Hempshaw End was the knowledge, garnered in from various impeccable sources, that the Goodwins were not paying their way. This might have been found amusing by that stratum of village society who were owed no money, had no money, and held no hopes of money. It was a different matter for the tradesmen, whose bills swelled to the point where even the laggard feudal courtesies of the Hemp Valley had to give way to warning stances. Many were impoverished by the standard of living that they had enabled the Goodwins to lead, a few of them totally ruined. And it was rumoured that there were incomparably weightier debts owed to creditors more commercially minded than the Lancashire–Yorkshire border folk. The word was whispered that there were last-ditch borrowings from the private bankers of a world of which the Hemp Valley knew nothing.

In Hempshaw End, Georgina said, men and women took pride in the independence of their judgement; though all that this meant was that they were as conventionally narrow, as socially envious, and as mindlessly xenophobic as the natives of any other valley. At the bottom they were contemptuous of the Goodwins. They firmly believed that in Hempshaw End they knew what was what. They knew that one day the Goodwins would come unstuck. And unstuck was what they came. Second mortgages, irredeemable, came up for redemption. Foreclosure was inevitable. The Hempshaw End estates were sold off and the Goodwins—Janie included—disappeared from Hempshaw End.

After they had gone, Hempshaw End did not hear

regular, precise news of them. They went to settle in a
part of the country that was not even a reality to
Hempshaw End. But the news that did come to them
from time to time suggested that the Goodwins were
not doing too badly. The son had got into the headlines
in an interesting social scandal: there were still occa-
sional adventuresses from the lower orders who took
chances with young men who looked as if their families
might be in the money. And those had certainly been
the appearances that young Goodwin kept up. One
would have thought that primogeniture would have
been little more than a token in the lives of the Goodwins. What is the point of managing property intact for
the monopoly of the eldest son when there is nothing to
monopolize? Nevertheless, the committal of all eggs to
one basket was a concept natural to the family temperament. The Goodwins were always scrupulous about
form, even where content was lacking. And perhaps the
relic of the family fortunes was a good deal greater than
the Official Receiver had ever got to hear about. If
young Wilson Goodwin was leading the sort of life that
Hempshaw End heard of him leading, it was clear that
something must have been retrieved. But the rest of
the Goodwin offspring had had to fend for themselves.
The girls—except for Janie—had fought desperately to
make sound marriages, which one or two of them actually did. But none of them achieved Janie's marital
distinction.

Janie must have been something near the twenty
mark when the Goodwins left Hempshaw. The property was sold to a Manchester unit-trust broker, who
sold it to a whizz-kid solicitor, who lost personal interest in it when his fiancée called off their marriage. And
so the estate eventually changed hands again, being
bought by the County Education Committee, who trans-
formed it into a Field Studies Centre. Hence the two
parties of students whom the two ladies had seen in the
cutting of the Old Railway that morning.

And to the surprise of those who had not forgotten

her, Janie Goodwin had come back to Hempshaw End.
Janie had always been known as the sport of the family,
not because she had fun—though that, too—but in the
sense that a botanical specimen will sometimes show
itself to be at variance with its genus. Janie was the only
Goodwin who managed to get herself well known in the
village. Even in her very early teens, she had seemed
to spend as much time on the corners of the village
streets as she did in the grounds of the Hall. There
were apocryphal tales of monumental reprisals against
her at home for her wilfulness. But opposition only
seemed to double her determination to strike out alone.

She was not made unreservedly welcome. The people she loitered about with were mostly about her own
age, and therefore less affected than their elders by the
vestiges of protocol. They laughed at Janie when she
was slow to understand their vulgarisms—and thought
of new and more striking vulgarisms with which to
broaden her horizons. They took pleasure in getting her
to say things disloyal to her home culture. And she kept
steadily coming back to them for more. The leggy girl
from the great debt-ridden house seemed fascinated
by what she saw outside the park gates. And there were
forces outside the park that saw her as a weapon with
which the arrogance of the big house might be assaulted.
She began to find one or two of the older people
indirectly and insidiously making "friends" with her.
She was invited into poorish homes for extravagant
north-country high teas: brawn and pigs' trotters, sa-
voury duck, mountains of bread and dripping—all of
which she wolfed as if they were on a starvation diet at
home. John William Cromwell's mother was one of the
hospitable ones, for some long-range and devious purpose of her own.

"We don't know," Georgina said, "what went on
between Janie and Noll when they were in their teens.
Tales are told, but I wouldn't rely on them. It's pretty
certain that Janie always did have a strong streak of
curiosity—and that Noll's seam of Rabelaisian coarse-

ness has been, if anything, mellowed by time. But the Goodwins left, not quite by moonlight, but in the moonlight spirit. And Hempshaw End lost individual track of them. Goodness knows, our London connection is tenuous enough even today. In the pre-war depression years, people might as well have been living on different continents."

Georgina got up, went to the window and looked out at the amorphous jumble of lighted village windows.

"Of course, you never thought of me as someone who had north-country connections—or even north-country sympathies."

"I must say, it never occurred to me—to any of us."

"Well, don't look as if you'd have rejected me for it if you'd known. Between the Goodwins' going and Janie's coming back there was a gap of nearly thirty years. What she had been doing in the meanwhile, how she had passed the war, what sort of living she had made for herself—these are things that nobody knows—except, one presumes, Noll Cromwell—and he's never talked about her. It was about 1932 that she left. She returned in about '58, aged round the forty mark. I was still teaching in the south in those days. She was already dug in in her cottage when I came here."

She went and put logs on the fire.

"From all accounts, no one knew at first who she was. There were a lot of new faces in the village—not many who remembered the Goodwins—and even fewer who cared. Janie was just another from town, people thought, buying up village property, fancying the peasant life."

Georgina laughed.

"Like me. I bought the school, when the Authority said they had no further use for it. But, of course, the name Goodwin rang bells. And if people did not know her, she knew some people. She talked to them—not prying, but showing an unaccountable interest—and knowledge. And when someone at last nailed her down, she did not try to conceal who she was.

"But she would not talk about the rest of her family. She was always a strange woman. She took a penetrating interest in people, and yet she preferred them at a certain distance. I don't think she ever considered herself superior, but she liked to be one apart. She dressed peculiarly—long skirts with costume jackets, antediluvian button-boots, hats out of the ark. It wasn't at all, though, as if she had equipped herself at a jumble sale—there are plenty of people in Hempshaw End who do that. Everything Janie wore was in immaculate condition—but it was always at least seventy years behind cut and fashion. Not merely seventy years behind the fashion—she wore clothes that were seventy years old. I think she did it to cock a snook at conformity— the conformity of any class, of any period. You'd have thought to look at her that she was colour-blind, texture-blind, pattern-blind and impact-blind. But I'm sure that was all deliberate. It was to make doubly sure that no one missed her oddities. I don't know what grievances she was harbouring—but I think they were pretty bitter. She hit back by making it aggressively clear that she was her own person."

Georgina looked again out the window, this time as if something in the night outside had caught her attention. For a moment whatever movement it was held up her story. But presently she turned back into the room again.

"Then there followed this wild and eruptive friendship with Noll Cromwell. Love–hate: the cliché never had a more clinical illustration. There were nocturnal comings and goings between their two cottages; nobody pretended there was anything platonic about it—and people were delighted to be scandalized. She would noisily throw Noll out of her place in the middle of the night. More than once she came tearing furiously out of his. And yet they kept going steadily back to each other. I can't tell you, no one knows, all that really went on. Sometimes I wondered if they liked getting together just for the joy of fighting. Obviously, each was supplying something that the other needed. Noll

Cromwell was a builder who hadn't put a house up for years. He used to make coffins as a sideline, and became the man people turned to for funerals. His gravedigger obscenities were—*are*—out of this world—but that's another story. He pretended to take an ebullient joy in burying people. And somehow this suited the local temperament. People seemed to find something comforting, a sort of familiarity, in his grossness.

"Then Hempshaw End woke to find he was putting the footings in for a new cottage. He'd been down to Bradburn for planning permission. When it was finished, he and Janie were going to be married."

"And you were best man."

"I was indeed. A highlight in my life."

"You encouraged them."

"My dear child, you say that as if I were doing something irresponsible. What world are you living in? Would my disapproval have made a ha'porth of difference to Janie and Noll? I liked both of them—in a way. They were different. They had the nerve to be different—to be themselves. What if they did play now and then to a rowdy gallery? What if their eccentricities were as outrageous as they could make them? They were only showing what they thought of society. They needed each other, though what precisely it was that they did need in each other, God only knows. Yes: I encouraged them—but that did not make them my responsibility. They were master and mistress of their own fate. And even over the brink, they scrambled back. I think they realized before they reached their front door that they could never live together."

"And now she's dead—isn't she?"

"I'm afraid it looks horribly like it."

"And he killed her?"

"How can he have? Mosley was mowing his lawn. Noll Cromwell was pinned down in his own house over the whole of the operative time. I suspect that Mosley knew something. And I don't somehow think that he is very far from Hempshaw End at this moment."

5

Beamish scanned the map as if there might be something in the greens and browns that could tell him where Mosley was. There were isolated farms with defiant names, clinging to narrow contour-lines and reached by trails of faint dots that were alleged to be footpaths: Starvelings, Stony Acre, Whistling Jack's. Sometimes the theoretical roads stopped for no ascertainable reason in the middle of unpopulated valleys. The blue meanders of moorland trickles emerged, merged, and in some cases came absurdly to an abrupt end. *Sawmill. Ruins. Ford.* Square mile upon square mile of storm-ruffled heather, a resilient stubble of bilberries. *Inn. Post office. Old mineshafts.* Mosley's country.

And where, in this wilderness peopled by cranks, scarecrows and red-faced, bull-necked defiers of the elements, was Mosley likely to be found? Why should Mosley, on his precious annual leave, be lingering in surroundings where he was likely to be trapped back into work at any moment: work which he did not want to become involved in—officially?

Grimshaw had ordered Beamish to find Mosley, and Beamish liked to be seen achieving the impossible. He drove out of Hempshaw End not entirely at random. Mosley must have gone uphill. If he had gone downhill, he would have passed Janie's cottage while the women were parked outside it—or very soon afterwards, perhaps while Miss Crane was rushing round looking for him. They would have run into him. He could not have helped becoming involved at once. Presumably Mosley on leave would be using his car, a specimen Ford Popular which he stubbornly refused ever to drive on duty.

So Beamish opted for uphill. He drove up the narrow road that flanked the Cotter Edge escarpment, where the principal traffic hazard was an unexpected sheep round a blind corner. In about three miles he reached the unaccountable hamlet of Barker's Clough, six houses deposited without symmetry or any imaginable purpose where the road dipped to a splashing brook. One of the houses had turned itself into a rudimentary shop, even bore a metal placard proclaiming itself to be the parcels agency of a bus service that had stopped running in the 1930s. Beamish pulled off the road and went in to buy something for a snack lunch, found biscuits and a box of processed cheese. He asked if any other travellers had been through recently. The woman behind the counter looked at him as if she did not believe in giving information to strangers.

"I was thinking of a stubby little man. Black hat. Raincoat."

"Do you mean Mr. Mosley?" A faint smile seemed about to raise the corners of the woman's mouth, but she disciplined it at once. "Are you a friend of his, then?"

"I *am* a police officer."

Another faint flicker stirred her eyes and mouth—but this time it was a ripple of uncertainty.

"He's on holiday," she said.

Did everyone, even in the remotest corners of this bleak end-of-world, know the fine details of Mosley's life? Had every man, woman and child on this hillside a brooding loyalty to Mosley?

"I'm not sure he'd thank me for having him disturbed."

Beamish, to whom it was unthinkable ever to be at a loss, was at a loss. One wrong word and this woman would become his enemy. And that would mean that within an hour or two, the whole tract would be enemy territory.

"I think you might find the opposite is true," he found himself saying, though he knew that such speech was formal and would probably be counter-productive.

"Oh, aye?"

The eyes scanning his face, disbelieving, yet hankering to believe, were prepared to obstruct him, yet by nature she was unwilling to offend.

"You're on holiday too, perhaps?" she suggested.

"That's right."

"And are you neighbouring too?"

"Neighbouring?" Was she asking him if he lived near here? Whatever she was getting at, she evidently hoped that he would say yes. He said yes.

"It's a wonderful job you men are doing—that neighbouring. Mr. Mosley's gone to clean up Emma Rawlings's windows for her. Then he was hoping there'd be daylight enough for him to go and do a bit of digging for Isaac Perry."

"I don't know either of them," Beamish said. "But I'll go and lend him a hand, if you'll tell me where I can find those people."

And that was how Beamish found his way to Widow Rawlings's home, a diminutive farmhouse that was no longer part of a diminutive farm. The widow was an octogenarian with the complexion of a withering apple. She also had a patent hostility to unknown quantities—of which Beamish was clearly one. It was his impression that it would take a couple of decades for anyone to earn a guarantee of her goodwill. Mosley had obviously been in her good books in his time—but he was in trouble with her today. She did not want him to do the work that he was doing for her, though to the *continuo* of her protests, he was simply getting on with it. He had not only cleaned her windows inside and out, upstairs and down, but had taken down her curtains and was at the moment washing them in her kitchen sink.

Her objections were implacable. She was put to shame by having all this done for her. And she was even more put out at having her windowpanes laid naked, even though there was no habitation from which they could be observed.

Mosley at the sink was a sight for a connoisseur. He had taken off his raincoat—in itself a rare event—and even his jacket, exposing the shiny back of his waistcoat. He had rolled up his shirt-sleeves and was wringing out the heavy material with his hands. But he still had his hat on, the Anthony Eden model, which he wore without any nuance of chic or verve.

"I'll pin blankets up at the windows before I go," Mosley told the old woman. "And Mr. Beamish here will be round very early in the morning to take them down for you and put your curtains back up. If you are nice to him, he might even iron them for you. I can't come myself, because I've promised old Neddy Wardle I'll plant his cabbages out."

Mosley must have been observing Beamish's final approach for several minutes. He did not turn to pay proper attention to him now. Beamish had no idea at all what the chances were that he would be free to come back here tomorrow.

"Just doing an afternoon's sightseeing, then, Beamish, are you?" Mosley asked, cheerful and casual, the look in his eye demanding an answer in the affirmative.

"I thought I'd have a look round between jobs," Beamish said brightly. "Got a busy week, for a man on leave, haven't you?"

"I'm neighbouring," Mosley said. "Easter to Whitsuntide, that's our main season. It's a little organization that a few of us have got together. There'd be room for you in it. We need young blood—and muscle. Bit of spring-cleaning here, turn over the top soil there."

"Mow an undertaker's lawn now and then?"

But Mosley did not rise to that one in any way.

"I might consider lending a hand now and then," Beamish said.

Mosley moved back from the sink to carry the curtains out to the clothes-line. Beamish was in his way, stepped back and got in Emma Rawlings's way instead. He followed Mosley into the yard, stepped among the relics of the former farm: a corroded milk churn, a broken pump.

"Mr. Mosley—who's offering a gallows on the open market?"

"Keep your voice down. She's not as deaf as she makes out."

Then, loud enough for her to be certain to hear, Mosley said, "I'll put your name forward. And if you'd care to anticipate election to the Neighbours by giving me a bit of help this weekend, I could certainly do with it."

"Whose gallows?" Beamish whispered, as loud as he dared.

"Billy Birkin's. Hempshaw Fold."

"What does anyone want with a gallows in Hempshaw Fold?"

"Practice," Mosley said.

"So why's he selling it? Has he had practice enough? Does he feel he's got all the skills he needs now?"

"Not much call for that sort of talent, down in the Fold."

"Come to think of it, we don't hear of many executions on your patch. Of course, that might just be a case of bad communications. Did you know there's been trouble today in Hempshaw End?"

"That had nothing to do with Billy Birkin."

Mosley disappeared suddenly round the other side of the curtain that he was hanging out. Beamish followed him.

"Billy's fair boiling over with resentment," Mosley said. "He feels he's never had a chance."

"I dare say there are some in Hempshaw Fold who are grateful for that."

"Not that Billy was ever keen on hanging folk. It was

his mother's idea. Go in and ask old Emma if she's got any more clothes-pegs, will you?"

When he came back, Mosley played Box and Cox with him several times round the clothes-line, then stood captive a moment.

"Of course, I've never met Billy Birkin's mother," Beamish said.

"She always wanted Billy to apply for the job of assistant hangman—when he was a youngster, that is. She used to say that every man ought to learn a useful trade."

"Albert Pierrepoint got his redundancy money years ago."

"That's why Billy's selling up—this latest vote in Parliament. He's given up hope, you see. His mother had made him put in for it, in the days when there were vacancies. She said the job would make a man of him. And he was sent for interview, but he didn't do too well at the tests that they put him through."

Mosley put a clothes-peg in his mouth, which did not make his croaking whisper any easier to catch.

"Billy couldn't bring himself to pull the lever, you see—even when it was only a dummy on the trap. He was too nice, that was the whole trouble. Too mild a man. Then he got into difficulty with the Home Office Weight Tables. When they asked him a test question, about what sort of a drop he'd give a man of nine stone three, he worked it out at forty-five feet. So he wasn't taken on."

"And his mother had the gallows made so that he could get into the way of it, and try again?"

"That's right. Noll Cromwell put it together for her: beautiful job—counter-weights just so, thirteen steps up, handrails for the screws to hold on to. But this last free vote in the Commons has knocked the stuffing right out of Billy. Hence the sale."

"Superintendent Grimshaw and the Assistant Chief Constable are very anxious to know whether anybody's made an offer for it yet."

"Oh, yes—there've been several. Seller's market."

"Who?" Beamish almost shouted, then asked again, a mere flutter of breath, "Who?"

"Billy's thinking of letting it go to Sarah Bramwell."

"I see. And do you know whether Sarah Bramwell has any specific activity in mind?"

"Well, it's a consortium, really. Sarah, Millie Hunter, Peggy Norton. But it's Sarah's money: she's only letting the others have nominal shares. Sarah took her lump sum out of the Sick and Divide Club at the Hempshaw Fleece last week."

"And what use do these ladies propose to put a gallows to?"

"Re-enactments, Sunday mornings, in Sarah's shed. Crippen first, Bywaters and Thompson coming up—that will obviously be a double bill, probably an Easter special. Private showings only of course. The Vigil Aunties, they call themselves. Not very funny," Mosley conceded.

"Harmless, I suppose."

"Compared with some things that are happening— and are likely to happen in the near future."

If this was a veiled acknowledgement of current events, it was the first that Mosley had made.

"Mind you, if you've got an hour or two to spare, I dare say this gallows business would bear looking into. Billy's still considering Sarah's offer. There are others in the field. I may not know about them all. And it's not the sort of apparatus I'd care to see fall into the wrong hands."

"I'll pass that on to Grimshaw. He wants to see you, by the way."

"I was afraid he might. You'd better tell him I don't see how it's possible. I'm just filling in with a little neighbouring, waiting for a standby flight to Nairobi. I've a sister out there, you know."

"Will you be able to get a flight back in time for the end of your leave?"

"I dare say."

"I'll certainly *tell* him that . . ."

So if Grimshaw started importuning Mosley, Mosley had his escape-story tidily ready? Even so, there was nothing in his tone that made the Nairobi story sound at all probable.

"But in the meanwhile, Mr. Mosley—"

In the meanwhile, Beamish had better extract something coherent to take back to Grimshaw. But at the moment they were interrupted by the arrival of Emma Rawlings, who wanted one of her less reputable curtains moved to where it could not be seen from the road.

"Seriously, Beamish—neighbouring. It's only in the spring and early summer that we mount a really intensive campaign. But one or two of us are always on call for emergencies—like humping coal, unstopping drains, or even doing a bit of shopping, if somebody's off-colour. How about it?"

"I'll think about it."

"I'll tell you what—I've got a lot on my hands this next day or two: that's if I'm not suddenly called off to Kenya. If I tell you where I'm likely to be, could you drop round and lend me a hand, if you can get yourself free?"

Beamish wondered whether he was getting the right message out of all this. Was it an invitation to stay in touch generally?

"Tomorrow morning I shall be in Hadley Dale, teaching Steve Blamire to ride a bike. That's a long-standing promise."

"Got no father, hasn't he? No uncles?"

"Not for some time now. He's sixty-seven. But he's always wanted to get going on two wheels. Tomorrow afternoon, dig Walter Needham's patch. Sunday morning I'm taking two old ladies to chapel in Higher Stoneley. I shall stop for a pint in the Angler's Arms when I've run them home again."

Beamish worked like a mental dynamo to memorize the detail.

"Sunday afternoon's free so far. There's no telling what might have blown up by Sunday afternoon."

Mosley had now rearranged the clothes-line to Emma Rawlings's satisfaction, and she was on her way back indoors.

"Mr. Mosley," Beamish said. "Superintendent Grimshaw—"

"Far be it from me to come between Grimshaw and his pleasures."

"Superintendent Grimshaw has a pipe that he thinks belongs to you."

Mosley patted his pocket, as if he had so far not missed it. Beamish handed it to him to examine, and he put it in his mouth immediately.

"It *is* yours, is it?"

"Oh, aye."

"Do you know where it was found, Mr. Mosley?"

Mosley looked inanely vacant.

"In Janie Goodwin's garden," Beamish said.

This did not seem to strike Mosley as in any way a grave matter.

"Mr. Mosley—perhaps you don't know what's happened today at Janie Goodwin's?"

Beamish gave him a succinct account, to which Mosley listened without excitement.

"I'm not quite sure I understand," he said, when Beamish had finished. "You say there was a fish in the window?"

"Yes—the fish is a symbol of—"

"Yes—I do know about that. But when is the fish supposed to have been put there? Is the man who wrecked the room supposed to have left it to draw convenient attention to himself? Or is Janie supposed to have put it there after she'd been hit on the head with a bottle?"

"I don't think anybody's followed up that line of thought."

"It all sounds a bit fishy to me." Mosley cackled

idiotically. "It'll give Grimshaw something to cudgel his brains with, won't it?"

"Mr. Mosley—are you sure you don't know anything about what's being going on in Hempshaw End?"

Mosley shook his head solemnly. "I'm on leave," he said.

There was a danger signal in his tone. Beamish knew from experience that once Mosley felt driven to consolidate, you might as well give up all hope of digging him out again.

"Tomorrow, Sergeant Beamish, if you can see your way to meeting me somewhere, perhaps you'll be able to bring me up to date about all this. I'd hate to think that anything untoward has happened to Janie Goodwin."

"I'll do my best," Beamish said. "And it's not for me to express opinions. You're an older man than I am, Mr. Mosley—but can you go on ignoring Mr. Grimshaw?"

"I've been doing nothing else for years."

Emma Rawlings's shrill voice called from the farmhouse kitchen door, telling them that she had just mashed a pot of tea. She sounded as if this were some punishment she was meting out to them for the upheaval of her domestic peace. That signalled the end of tactical discussion between Mosley and Beamish. Beamish stayed long enough for common courtesy—not that Mrs. Rawlings let herself be seen to be influenced by that— then drove back to Hempshaw End to look for Grimshaw.

During the course of the previous case that they had worked on together, Beamish had at intervals believed that he was beginning to understand Mosley.

6

I did not think that Georgina would ever be ready for bed. She simply could not stop talking and I had to sit straight-faced pretending to be enthralled—and becoming more befogged as each quarter-hour passed. I completely fail to understand the love of vulgarity that seems to have taken possession of her.

"I grant you the man is gross," Georgina said. "But you'll have to take my word for it: when it comes to coarseness, he is well past his prime. There was a time when he was matchless. I think he is getting too tired to be as offensive as he used to be."

"It's people's fault for putting up with him."

"But don't you see, Elizabeth—people like it? He has never done anybody any harm. His vulgarity is cathartic —it purges the soul of other emotions. There was a time, when his business was in full swing, when he had the monopoly of funerals for miles around, when he *lived* the part. Even hale and hearty people weren't free from his banter. He would go about assessing people's weight, asking them for their measurements, telling them they all had to pass through his hands in the end. Little Madge Mason, at the post office—her husband

46

stood six feet seven in his socks, and every time he saw her, Noll used to say, 'Don't forget, Madge, send over and let me know any time your Walter's feeling at all seedy. I shall have to get an extra length of pine for his box.'

"But old Emma Rawlings—that's the richest tale in his repertoire. Noll always used to take pride in getting a smile out of the bereaved before they'd left the church-yard. He used to say that was included in his estimate, but he knew in advance that Emma was going to be a challenge to him. Emma never was by nature the smil-ing type. He said he knew he'd have to be satisfied if he could get her to bare her teeth for him.

"And that turned out to be the trouble: her teeth. He just couldn't say anything that would get her to curl her lips back. All his usual little quips failed. She went back to her house in faceless misery—and Noll wasn't much happier, feeling he'd not come up to his self-appointed standards. 'If they don't get over the worst of it at the graveside,' he used to say, 'happen they never will.'

"Then that evening there came a knock at his door, and he saw Emma Rawlings standing out there in the dark, looking at him with a mixture of pleading and despair.

"'Come on in, Emma,' he told her. 'How have you got here? It's good six miles from Barker's Clough.'

"'I've walked it,' she said. 'I don't know whether I'm too late.'

"Normally Noll would have said that, short of offering to bring her husband back, there was nothing he wouldn't have a go at. But he judged that that wasn't quite the approach for this occasion. Emma's troubles were more practical than that.

"'It's me teeth,' she told him."

Georgina rather fancied herself at the dialect. Eliza-beth found it degrading.

"'Your teeth? I've got a book on dentistry up on the shelf, but I'm not halfway through it yet. Of course, I'll tackle anything to oblige.'

" 'I know you will, Noll. But I'm not sure you can manage this—have you filled our Sam in yet?'

" 'Oh, aye. I always like to get the filling-in done before nightfall. People have enough to contend with, without getting up in the morning to catch sight of an open hole.'

" 'But they've buried my teeth with him.'

"And Noll said it was a fact that he thought Sam had looked fuller-faced in death than he had done latterly in life—his mouth and cheeks less sunk in.

" 'He'd borrowed them to bite on a bit of toast-crust he'd asked me for, just before he went. And with all the fuss that followed, and me being off my food, I forgot to get them back. It isn't the money that worries me, Noll, it's all the bus rides to Bradburn, and my mouth full of plaster, then the hanging about, and all the soreness waiting for the new lot to settle down.'

" 'Not to worry, Emma. You'll have your own set back by morning.'

"And she did. That's the sort of man he is, Elizabeth. Those are the lengths he would go to for a friend or customer. He dug Sam up, and he filled him in again, and he had those dentures over at Barker's Clough by sunrise. As he told Emma, she'd have faded away from starvation if she'd had to wait for a Home Office Exhumation Order.'

"That's the most disgusting story I've ever listened to," Elizabeth Stirrup said.

7

By the time that Beamish got back to Hempshaw End, Grimshaw had set up the beginnings of a Report Centre on classical lines in the village hall. The one-inch map was pinned to a table-top, and the staff at the moment consisted of a uniformed sergeant in charge of the filing system, which so far consisted of one clipboard.

"You found Mosley."

Beamish answered with a slight nod. He had given a good deal of thought to how much or how little he would have to tell Grimshaw. The only conclusion he had come to was to play things as they came.

"Where was he?"

"In Barker's Clough, sir."

That was safe enough. Mosley would be well clear of Barker's Clough by now.

"And what the hell was he doing in Barker's Clough?"

"Neighbouring, sir."

"I don't know what that means."

"Actually, he was laundering an old woman's curtains for her, to her considerable dismay. Mosley belongs to a club that eases old people out of winter into spring. I rather think that he's a foundation member."

"Yes, yes."

Grimshaw was testy. He was clearly up against frustration on all fronts. One of his difficulties was going to

49

be to raise the manpower that he could see himself needing.

"Your orders were to tell him to report to me, Beamish."

"He's standing by for a flight to Africa, sir."

"Africa?"

Grimshaw looked at him through narrowed eyes, as if he suspected him of treachery.

"That's what he said, sir."

"And you believe him, I suppose?"

"That's what he said."

"And what did he say about what has happened here?"

"Very little, sir. It wasn't clear whether he knows anything about it or not."

"*Does* he, Beamish? Does he know anything or doesn't he? You're not going to tell me that you couldn't make your mind up."

Beamish hesitated. His loyalty to Mosley, after all, had to depend on crosswinds. He felt that Mosley had shown only limited loyalty to him.

"I think he probably does, sir."

Then Beamish brightened. He remembered that he had at least achieved part of his assignment.

"I have found out whose gallows have come on to the market, sir."

Billy Birkin and Sarah Bramwell; Crippen—and the double bill for Easter: Beamish made everything that could be made out of the story—a good deal more than Grimshaw had patience with. It was as an afterthought, after Grimshaw believed he had got him away from the subject, that Beamish added, "And I believe they call themselves the Vigil Aunties, sir."

"You are working in collusion with Mosley, aren't you, Beamish? You're on his side, aren't you?"

"No, sir."

"You had better be, Beamish. He is your superior officer."

"Sir—it is less than fair to put me in a situation in which—"

"You are not being put in any situation, Beamish. What do you think this is—an employment agency? This is a police force, and I sent you to liaise with Mosley. He is on to something, isn't he?"

"I rather think he is, sir."

"He is actively pursuing it."

"That was my impression, on balance."

"Under cover of these geriatric good works?"

"I gather that he is usually fairly busy in that direction at this time of year, sir. He was hoping that I would be able to lend him a hand with some of his tasks over the next day or so."

"He really thinks I can spare you to help him to mow lawns, with all the flap that there will be going on here?"

"He merely expressed the hope, sir."

"You sound like Jeeves. Mosley is a fool, Beamish."

Beamish was silent.

"I have heard many men say that, Beamish. I have said it myself. Once or twice in his career—just once or twice—he has turned the tables on us. I do not trust him, Beamish. The question is—is this one of Mosley's genuine brainstorms? Beamish—give me some sort of answer."

"It is difficult to be sure, sir."

"I have no doubt that you and Mosley have made surreptitious arrangements to contact each other?"

"If you wished me to speak to him again, sir, I do not think it would be too difficult for me to find out whose plot he is digging at any given time. I believe he said something about teaching an elderly gentleman to ride a bicycle."

"What was that foolish word you used? Neighbouring? Do you fancy washing people's curtains and scraping out their rabbit hutches, Beamish?"

"I will turn my hand to anything in the path of duty, sir."

"Then turn it to neighbouring—tomorrow. But Beamish—I shall want to see you personally with a prog-

ress report tomorrow evening. Tomorrow is Saturday.
We will consider Sunday's deployment in the light of
whatever you have to tell me."

"Sir."

8

Some of the younger students at the Field Studies
Centre had never before been out in the true darkness
of night. All their lives they had been used to some
degree of street-lighting, or at least to the glimmer of a
curtained window illuminating concrete. The organizers
of the courses therefore had no difficulty in putting
together interesting night exercises for them. Almost
everything excited them—at least for the first ten
minutes—and almost everything was an event. Even as
mundane a necessity as a boy urinating against a tree in
the middle distance could be turned into an object
lesson on the way noise travels at night.

The scholars from St. Mary's Church of England
Primary School at Hepton Ford might be said to be
enjoying their field course vicariously. They had been
led to look at lichens and water beetles, they had filled
their pockets with pine cones and vacated snail shells,
they had looked at owl pellets through hand-lenses.
But for most of them this was a first experience of living
together away from home. The eight- and nine-year-
olds talked incessant sex, found corners for clandestine
smoking, and there was one little knot of girls for whom
life held no greater joy than to slip a quarter of a mile

behind the rest of the party and sing pop choruses in the shelter of a gritstone shooting-butt.

The older party staying at the Centre were a group of survey students from Bradburn Tech, and for them night was rather a different matter. They passed the day going through the motions of triangulating arbitrary parcels of the bleak landscape, and were supposed to spend at least part of their evenings putting their calculations on record. But they were not strangers to darkness, nor to its potential. They were six or seven years older than the group from the school, a gap which made a vital difference in orientation. For whereas the children talked of very little else but the facts of life, the students had reached the stage of practical work in that area too. And for a number of them, this expedition was providing a first real opportunity. The evening—and for one or two who had got things organized, the whole night—offered unrivalled chances for research and the supplementation of human knowledge. It even made it seem worthwhile slogging the hills for five hours a day in pursuit of trigonometrical ratios.

Nigel Teesdale and Sue Grayson, for example, were drifting by mutual expectation towards their first adult experience. They were both seventeen, and they both lived on the same tower-block estate on the developing perimeter of Bradburn. They had both been the sole reason why their parents had married, and each had at home a regular companion with whom they had so far shrunk from actual copulation.

Previously known to each other only by sight, they had discovered each other on this week's outing—as early, in fact, as the outward journey on the college minibus. After an hour or so of treating each other with a sort of comic contempt, they had thrown the sentiments of their native Bradburn to the winds and gone abundance on each other, under the impression that the manner of their courtship was highly original and exclusive to themselves. Sue tried a clumsily obvious middle course between playing hard to get and dropping un-

ambiguous hints that she might not prove impossible.
Nigel kept his eyes fixed on the main object of life by
steering the conversation whenever he could on to such
stimulating subjects as soft porn and the ethics of con-
traception. On the off chance, he had in fact equipped
himself for field-work by buying half a dozen packets
of an elementary device at his hairdresser's.

And tonight—the night of the Friday on which Janie
Goodwin had disappeared—he was going to go the
whole hog. Sue knew this—and though she had made
no promises, she had not allowed him to stray more
than a yard or two from her side throughout the day.

The boudoir of their Eden had already been ear-
marked: an old plate-layer's hut—a solid little building
with a low-pitched roof, which stood by the former
track of the Old Railway. There was something about
old railways—Georgina Crane surged with awareness of
it. They made her think of the journeys that had been
so vital to those who had made them. She thought of
red oil lamps flickering between the rear buffers of
disappearing trains. She thought of family partings, the
only memory of someone whisked away being a sprite
of smoke hung earthbound under the coping-stones of
silent bridges.

Sue and Nigel had no such thoughts. Their single-
minded conception of romance was enshrined in that
plate-layer's hut. The hut was in fact famous in the
mythology of the Field Studies Centre. Tales about the
role it had played in human relationships had been
passed on from one visiting party to another for years.

One difficulty tonight was that the party of Juniors
was being officially conducted along the Old Railway as
part of their nocturnal education. They had made loud,
crude jokes at the sight of the hut, of which they had
also heard. Some of them tried to get into it, only to
find that its door had been fitted with a new hasp and
padlock. It seemed an age before Nigel and Sue were
able to get near the place. By then it was almost too
late for them to avail themselves of its amenities. They

had almost reached the culmination of biological existence lying behind one of the broken walls of the cutting whilst the Juniors were still in earshot. But Sue did not care much for the scratchy stalks of the creeping bilberry shrubs against the sensitive skin on the insides of her thighs. And Nigel underwent a temporary loss of virility when a picnic-tamed sheep tried to nuzzle his bare posterior.

The schoolchildren eventually moved off to laugh, sing and urinate elsewhere. Sue and Nigel clambered down the embankment. Nigel removed the hasp and padlock, using the blade of his penknife as a screwdriver. He had a pocket torch with him, and shone it into the inside of the hut.

Sue gave a little yelp at what they saw. There was a smell of resinous timber in the hut, and a sort of raised platform had been erected in the middle of it. Its purpose was all too clear: a rope was hanging from a cross-beam, and a woman's body, dressed in old-fashioned clothes, was hanging from the rope, her waist at about the level of the open trap.

They closed the door and ran haphazard along the cutting, as if what they had seen could physically harm them. Then, smoking cigarettes in trembling fingers within comforting sight of the lights of the village, they discussed what they had found. They came to the conclusion that they could only make trouble and embarrassment for themselves by telling anyone about it.

"No, sir. I have been unable to trace him."

Detective-Superintendent Grimshaw was, neither by temperament nor discipline, an untruthful man, but some degree of disingenuousness seemed bound to creep in whenever he was compelled to discuss Mosley with the Assistant Chief Constable.

"Well, at least that's one hazard you're free of," the Assistant Chief Constable said.

"I wouldn't be so sure of that. Mosley is about. There are indelible signs that Mosley is about."

"Oh?"

"An allotment dug here, a hen house whitewashed there. Mosley appears to be lugging his social conscience about the fells."

"Good God!"

"However—it isn't Mosley that I'm concerned about." No mention of Beamish, not a reference to Barker's Clough—"What I am anxious about is the size of the army I am going to be able to muster to beat across the hills tomorrow at first light."

"You know very well the size of the army we can muster. What with Bradburn playing at home, minor royalty staying at Blendale Castle, and a Hell's Angels rally in Calesdale, I doubt whether I can rake up a dozen for you."

"You know, sir—this is hopeless."

But then an incoming phone call brought him inspiration. A party of children, out studying "The Sounds of the Countryside by Night," had discovered a pair of woman's knickers, clinging to a gorse bush on the moors a few hundred feet above Hempshaw End. They were apparently an outrageous outsize in woman's knickers, were untrimmed—aggressively plain, in fact—and were made in some coarse and heavy longcloth of a sort that had gone out of fashionable wear early in the century.

At least, Grimshaw knew now where he was going to recruit his army.

9

Dear Diary—Yes, I am in in such a state that I can write such a thing as that. It is the middle of the night, and I cannot find sleep. Georgina defeats me. My God, how can I ever have imagined myself in love with her? Throughout the evening, her eyes kept wandering to the window: not as if she were afraid of someone lurking out there, but as if she were expecting, positively *wanting* a visitor.

When we finally retired—I made a natural enough excuse to go up early—she seemed highly relieved. For some time after I had gone upstairs I could hear her moving about between the kitchen and the sitting-room. Then, straining my ears, I heard her quietly, secretively, open the back door. She let someone in—and I knew it was that man. But they kept their voices low. He has been in the house a couple of hours now, and I have not heard a word that has been said. But the horrible smell of his tobacco has filled the house and even crept under my bedroom door.

It is not that I want to conjure up afresh the foolishly imagined relationships of childhood. What distresses me is that all Georgina's sense of values seems to have been swept away by some hurri-

57

cane. Where is the Miss Crane who taught me
John Donne and *Lear*?

Georgina Crane knew that Noll Cromwell had been
hanging about outside for a long time, that he had been
waiting for Elizabeth Stirrup to go to bed. Because—
his coarseness apart—he was a man who would have no
difficulty in weighing up Elizabeth. It was a pity about
that child—unfair though it was, it was only as a child
that Georgina Crane could think of her. Had she been
in some form of spiritual hibernation since she had
come out of the last of her examination-rooms? It
made one think that it was too dangerous a responsibility by far, to risk trying to teach anybody anything.
What had Elizabeth Stirrup ever learned, beyond the
false values of A-Level Lit: a shopping-list of what to
look for in a work of art, which the examiners could
assess by a process of academic arithmetic.

Georgina went to her back-door and let Noll Cromwell in. He had dressed for the occasion—it would be
comic, if it were not so sincere a gesture on his part. He
was not quite in the funeral garb that the Valley expected of him. He had on his narrow-brimmed bowler,
a black suit with waistcoat and watch-chain—but not
the pigeon-fancier's medal that some said he had worn
at his wedding; and of course he had no black ribbons
fluttering from his hat-band. It was rather as if he had
got himself up to call on an old-fashioned solicitor.
The bottoms of his trousers fell over the eyelets of his
boots so that it was impossible to tell whether he was
wearing his knotted laces or not. It was unkind to look,
because Noll Cromwell was suffering. Beneath the sometimes terrifying image of the tearaway, Georgina always
thought of him as a saddened man who had never really
orientated himself.

"What can I offer you to drink? Coffee, cocoa—
something more bodisome?"

"If you told me you had whisky, I wouldn't say no to
it."

She had a drop of Scotch left in the cabinet.

"I'm going to share this between the two of us. I have a feeling we're going to get down to some basic truths tonight."

Cromwell looked too fatigued to rise to any verbal wit.

"What can you tell me, Miss Crane?"

"What can I tell you? Only what I found when I called to deliver Janie's dinner. I have no information at all that won't already have come your way."

"It's that silly bugger Mosley who's messed things up. I'm sorry, Miss Crane. I came here meaning to mind my manners, just for once."

"It doesn't matter, Mr. Cromwell. Only I never think that bad language does much to clarify things. In what sense do you think that Inspector Mosley has blundered?"

"All that about mowing my lawn. What chance had he of making any sort of a job of it? He knew something was going on—and he was determined to keep me out of it. Yet I can't think for a moment that he really knew what was going to happen. Whatever it was, it must have got out of hand."

"But what sort of thing can Mr. Mosley possibly have known?"

"I've been breaking my brains against that ever since the Superintendent came to see me. I can only think that Mosley knew that someone had come into the district whom it wouldn't be healthy for certain people to see."

"I've come to more or less the same conclusion myself. So have you any idea who it might be?"

"I haven't an inkling, ma'am. Janie, you know, she's been to places and done things in her time that you and I know nothing about."

"I'm sure she has. But if we're right about this, whoever it was would obviously be no stranger to you. Otherwise why would Mr. Mosley be going to such peculiar lengths to keep you out of trouble? If that's what you really think he was doing—"

"I'm sure it was."

"He wanted to keep me out of trouble. Maybe if I'd been there, there'd have been no trouble."

"Or maybe you'd have been under arrest by now for doing grievous bodily harm."

"Better that, than that Janie should have been hurt."

"So how many people out of your past and Janie's would you have done grievous bodily harm to, Noll?"

It was the first time in her life that Georgina had ever called him by his Christian name. She did not know why she had let it happen and for some seconds she was uneasy about the ill-wisdom of it. One never quite knew with these revolutionaries: they were so often deeply conventional at heart. But Noll Cromwell was so exclusively absorbed in his own thoughts that he seemed not to have noticed.

"So somebody may have come to seek Janie out," Georgina said. "From which phase of her life would you expect that to be?"

Significantly, Cromwell embarked on an oblique answer. "It's hard to say. Her childhood, you know—I'm speaking now of all the Goodwin kids, except the boy—it was not at all what you might have expected it to be."

"No. I've always heard that."

"He was a right old bugger, you know, was old Wilson Goodwin. Well, he must have been, mustn't he, to have had all those kids when, if the truth were told, they never could make ends meet? Well, for example, they weren't regular church-goers and I'd put him down as just about the most unchristian man in Hempshaw at that time—but if he decided that one particular Sunday they *were* going to church, then it was like putting the family on parade. He'd line them up in the entrance hall, and inspect each one of them from top to toe before he led them down the steps. Then they used to have to follow him, a respectful half a yard behind him, all the way to the church. He'd play merry hell if one of them had scuffed the toe of his boot. They went in fear and trembling of him when he was in that mood."

Cromwell paused. This was not exactly what he had intended telling. But Georgina eased him along. She knew which way his mind was working.

"Yes—I've heard that he was a capricious martinet."

In some ways, she probably knew more about the Goodwins than Cromwell did. They were talked about by other people, besides the villagers. Wilson Goodwin must have come into funds of some kind during his youth, which had enabled him to capitalize the things he thought he had lined up for himself and his family. Goodwin had suffered delusions of facile grandeur of a kind that was almost a cliché. As one of the most extensive landowners in the Hemp Valley, he expected facile success. Even an eventual title was not impossible if he did enough affluent entertaining of the right kind. There were some who said that what he longed for was a relatively impoverished Lord Lieutenant whom he could help out in his obligations. But the County, as everyone in the Valley could have predicted, never did let him in: presumably the unofficial standing committees did not take long over their enquiries. For the sake of showing what hospitality he could rise to, he had to fill the Hall over long weekends with townee freeloaders who cost him more than money: the very sight of them swanning about the countryside proved that the County had been right about him. And money was something which, over the first few years, he seemed remarkably capable of organizing on a strictly short-term basis; or, at least, he knew how to shift debts about. (One year, for example, he gained himself a wave of much-needed local popularity by putting the Hempshaw End cricket team on its feet, only to leave them to discover after the débâcle that they had the bills to settle for themselves.)

He had made an attempt to get into politics, having found a distant constituency purblind enough to adopt

him. (In the early stages, Goodwin always seemed able
to convince strangers of his charm, even of his financial stability.) But once he was let loose in a by-election,
he rapidly became the despair of his agent, pressing a
policy that was his own natural philosophy, an "England for the English" slogan, bluntly racist along a
pattern that even lacked epigrams, and aggressively
against any kind of namby-pamby collectivist social
concern. His basic incapacity—in effect, it was pure lack
of judgement—was a gift to an opponent who was not
without intellect, and within ten days of campaigning
he had become an embarrassment to many of his own
party, losing a safe seat on the second recount. He was
never invited to stand elsewhere. A similar sort of fate
seemed to befall every attempt that he made to replen-
ish his coffers by commercial ventures. Hempshaw End
was not well informed about the details, but he was
believed to have dabbled at one time in seaside holiday
bungalows, and at another in an infallible syndicate for
staking substantial cross-double racing bets. In such
enterprises he showed a flair for publicity, but it was on
a lavish scale that the projects proved unable to sustain.
And it was the local domestic suppliers of the Hall who
were the first to be disillusioned when he had to start
shunting his limited assets about: Frank Turner, Jimmy
Edmunds and Walter Slack.

"But it was the brother," Noll Cromwell said. "It was
only the brother that mattered to either of the parents.
I don't know what happened to young Wilson Goodwin.
Janie never knew, either."

There were certain things that Wilson Goodwin had
understood. One was how to control a sinking fund that
was beyond the reach—indeed beyond the knowledge—
of the receivers in bankruptcy. The other was the principle that estates, however unpromising, stand an obviously better chance of growth if they are kept intact.

"I've never understood how they managed it," Georgina Crane said. "There wasn't anything to be salvaged,
was there?"

"I don't understand it either, Miss Crane, and I don't think Janie ever did. For that matter, neither did the Fraud Squad—you can bet they must have taken more than a surface interest. There must have been holdings that did not stand up to be counted among the assets. They must have used a nominee—someone they knew they could trust—"

"That's something else that I've never understood, either—how the nominee system works. What's to stop any nominee with red blood in his veins from running away with the lot?"

Cromwell assumed a cunning look—not difficult for him, since when he was himself, he was certainly the most cunning man over a wide radius.

"There's more than one kind of hold you can have over a man."

"You mean blackmail?"

"Blackmail—fear—physical and worse—"

"So everything that was salvaged went to the son?"

"The girls were a sore disappointment to their father. He'd thought that they were going to turn out to be angels of culture and grace—the most sought-after young ladies on the marriage market. I think there must have been a lot about Wilson Goodwin that wasn't far above simple-minded. It certainly didn't work out that way. Where the hell did he think they were going to get their culture and grace from, that's what I want to know. As it turned out, a couple of them did marry men with handles to their names, but they were the sort who had to work for a living—not what you and I would call aristocracy, Miss Crane . . ."

He looked at her as if he did not doubt that she shared his social outlook. He seemed unaware that there might be anything incongruous in his sitting there expressing confidently final judgements on the quality of blue blood.

"At least, your Janie used to make her escape now and then," Georgina said.

"You mean the way she used to sneak out and smoke Woodbines with us behind Tommy Scragg's garage? Yes—even when she was no more than thirteen or fourteen, Janie had had her fill of that household. She could see right through them."

"And couldn't her sisters?"

"They were different. There wasn't one of them with Janie's guts or wit. They were taken up by all sorts of internal intrigues, which kept them fully occupied. It all bored Janie stiff. So she used to come out and muck about with us. That's how it all started."

Cromwell's eyes now were looking out into some personal remoteness.

"Yes. I was sweet on her right from the start. And my mother used to ask her into the house at meal times. That was not for the good of anybody's soul, I might tell you. My mother had an infinite capacity for mischief-making. She even knew how to invest in mischief for the future."

He laughed.

"Not that anybody would ever have taken us for sweethearts. We were at each other's throats even in those days. 'William Cromwell, you disgust me,' she used to say to me. 'Don't you have a mirror in your house? I suppose you'd be frightened of looking into it if you had. When did you last shampoo your hair? And you're going to lose all your teeth before you're much older.' "

Noll Cromwell looked solemn.

"I've not given up hope yet, you know. That's if nothing has happened to her."

The thought sent him into an internal spasm of helpless rage.

"If I find—"

Georgina hurried to interrupt him. "And Janie completely lost track of her brother?"

"To all intents and purposes. She has an idea that he got to be something during the war—a Major, or something of that sort. Then he went overseas—she thinks it might have been to South America. You can bet it would be somewhere where the sun shines, and where he doesn't have to work with his hands."

"And you really think that if he turned up round here for some reason, she might do something impetuous?"

"I don't know what to think."

"Don't you think that Janie would be above that sort of reaction nowadays?"

"She never talked much to me about her brother but I never cared for the look that came into her eyes when she did."

Georgina gave it some seconds' thought.

"But is all this something that Mr. Mosley would know anything about? We are talking on the assumption that his fingers are probing into this somewhere. Inspector Mosley wouldn't be in a position to recognize Janie's brother, would he?"

"I wouldn't have thought so. But I gave up thinking I knew anything about the working of Jack Mosley's mind a long time ago."

"And I wouldn't claim to know everything about the working of yours, either, Noll Cromwell. You've something else on it, haven't you?"

Cromwell was clearly now less at his ease. She thought he was on the threshold of the subject that he had really come here to discuss, and now that the actual moment had arrived, he was reluctant about it. Georgina thought it best not to try to prompt him again at this stage.

"Aye, well—there was another thing—another time in her life. Like all the Goodwin girls, there came a day when she'd her living to earn. Not that Janie was work-scared, you understand—but it had to be something that wouldn't sully the family name: not waitressing, or a shop counter, or anything where folk might come across her. She'd been sent to one of those jumped-up schools—oh, not a boarding place—there wasn't money

for that for the girls, that was reserved for young
Wilson—a private school on the outskirts of Bradburn,
a snob place if ever there was one. They'd filled her up
to her earholes with who she was supposed to be, and
what she was supposed to do about it. It made Janie
sick. And yet . . ."

Cromwell spread his hands in disavowal of values
that he could not countenance.

"I suppose if you're exposed to something often enough
and for long enough, something of it will rub off on
you."

There were differences between himself and Janie
that he still resented. Georgina could not help wondering if he held it against her that she had retained a
preference for some degree of personal cleanliness.

But immediately he was moved by his indestructible
sense of fairness to correct himself. "No—what am I
saying? There *was* something special about Janie. It was
in her bloodstream. I was telling you, she had to do
something to make herself self-supporting, and what
she did was to get taken on as companion by one of
those old biddies who are rolling in it. When she first
took the job, she did not mean to stay long in it—just
long enough to see if there was anything in it for her. If
she found she couldn't stand the old girl, she wasn't
going to stay at all. She'd play it as it came. It did at
least get her away from home. There was some talk that
they'd be spending part of each year abroad—and Janie
saw possibilities in that. She'd get herself somewhere
worth being, fare paid, then cut herself loose, according
to what opportunities she spotted. That wasn't the way
things worked out. As you probably know, she stayed
with the old girl for years—including the war."

Georgina did not know that. To the best of her knowledge, no one in Hempshaw End other than Cromwell
did know where Janie had spent that interim period.

"Lady Rimmington, that was her name. She seems to
have been a ripe old bird. Not that Janie ever really
told me much about her—and even when she was

talking, if ever she thought that I seemed to be listening a bit too attentively, she'd always shut up and start about something else. It was almost as if she felt afraid that I'd go getting the wrong idea. This Lady Rimmington was the widow of some starchy bloke who'd been somebody in the government service. And when he left her high and dry with enough to get by on, she seems to have come to the conclusion that she'd wasted enough of her life doing as she was told just to keep up government appearances. The time had come to please herself what she did with herself, and how she did it. And what she was looking for in a companion was someone to help her do just that—someone with an elastic attitude to things, someone young enough to be able to make a few spicy suggestions of her own—someone who'd encourage her to behave as if she were a youngster herself."

Cromwell flexed his upper limbs, as if his shoulder-blades were beginning itch under his Sunday suit.

"I'm not trying to say that they behaved as some of us might if we were let loose on the waterfronts of Europe with enough in the bank not to have to worry about paying by cheque. When it comes to kicking over the traces, a lot depends on what sort of a bearing-rein you've been held under up to now. It was a question of high living when they felt like it—or eating in a cheap café if it suddenly looked naughty enough to be interesting: which meant one that her husband would not have let her go into. They didn't spend enormous amounts of money in the long run, Janie always insisted, but if something did happen to catch their eye, then they'd go for it without having to face a sermon on extravagance. A flutter on the gaming-tables once in a while—then a liqueur too many after dinner if one of them had come up with a fifty-franc bonus. They travelled about Switzerland in the 1930s looking like *Punch* cartoons of English tourists—that's how Janie described them—getting their own way with everybody, because they looked so eccentric that nobody dared to thwart them."

Noll Cromwell had never been out of England in his life, but his reading had familiarized him with some unexpected backwaters—and so had some of the things that Janie had told him.

And another image came into Georgina's mind—a picture of Janie Goodwin in the absurdly old-fashioned clothes in which she used to go about Hempshaw End. Was this role-playing—the caricature English tourist in Interlaken—a copy-book maxim learned from Lady Rimmington? If so, it might well be that something had happened somewhere in upper-class holiday Europe that had had rather too abiding an effect on her. You couldn't help looking at Janie Goodwin and wondering if she were unhinged; yet you'd only to talk to her for five minutes to discover that she very patently wasn't.

"And for her years—the old girl was into her seventies—she was not beyond dolling herself up if there was a man in the offing whose company might help to while away an empty evening. That's the point that I'm coming to."

He paused to look Georgina straight in the eye, as if he felt the need to prove to her that he could look a fact in the face.

"Janie had her men-friends too. She never talked to me about them in so many words—but it stands to sense, doesn't it? And I do know that there was one who meant a lot to her. Well, again, it's what you'd expect, isn't it, in any girl of that age living that kind of life? But I've always had the feeling—one of those feelings that goes down inside a man's boots—that this man let her down—badly. This isn't the green eye, Miss Crane—how could it be, over something that happened when I wasn't in her life, anyway? But she's had a bad deal in a lot of places, has Janie Goodwin. She's been having bad deals all her life, and I've been one of them. But this was as rotten a blow as she ever took. It was one of those things that make an everlasting mark on a woman—on most women, anyway, I suppose.

There was a letter came for her one day, oh, five or six years ago, and she rushed to hide it away when she saw me coming in—not that I'd ever go poking about in her post, you understand—and she was irritable for the rest of the hour or so that I spent with her that day. Her mind wouldn't stay on everyday things, and it took her a day or two to get over it. I was on tenterhooks for a week or more—expecting something to happen, I didn't know what. I couldn't keep my eyes off the village streets, waiting for some stranger to arrive, someone who was going to deprive me of such of her company as I was still managing to get."

"You know, you *were* jealous, Noll."

"Of course I was. And even worse was wondering whether she might be persuaded to take herself off somewhere. It was a bad time, I can tell you."

Georgina was wishing that she had not finished off the Scotch in the only round she had poured.

"And now maybe she *has* taken herself off some-where—or been taken off—for better or for worse."

"Well, let's not make up our minds it's for the worse until we know, Noll."

It sounded hopelessly lame to her as she said it.

"I feel better now I've told you, Miss Crane. I know there's nothing either of us can do about it."

"I'm not so sure about that."

"What, then?"

He looked at her with pathetically childish anticipation of something miraculously optimistic. She wished she had not said it, but the need to offer some sort of solace had been strong.

"Well, you might try to get hold of Inspector Mosley, for one thing. You seem pretty sure that he knows more about all this than he'd care to admit—and I'm certain you're right."

"And where in hell's name is Mosley? He'll not be coming here in the open to sort the case out. He's on holiday."

"Oh, come, Noll—surely a man who knows this place and its people as well as you do could put his finger on Mr. Mosley in a couple of hours?"

The suggestion brightened up Cromwell perceptibly.

10

From the diary of Elizabeth Stirrup for Saturday, 9 April

I don't think I can bear to stay any longer in this village. There is a latent barbarism here that I would never have thought to find in twentieth-century England. I could hardly believe my eyes this morning when I saw children of eight or nine years old being paraded in the lane outside this house, prior to being led out in search of the corpse of the poor woman who was murdered yesterday.

As I saw them in their gaily-coloured, bobbed woollen caps, I wondered which of them would suffer the trauma of finding that body, badly bruised as it must be, to judge from the state we found that bottle in; probably hideously mutilated. And they were laughing and joking about it, as if it were some game they were going to play.

I told Georgina that I found it nauseating, but all she could find to say was, "Oh, they won't find her."

Georgina is out at the moment, organizing vil-

lage women to cut sandwiches for the large and
uncouth search-party that has been recruited.
Hempshaw End has entered into this as if it were
their annual fête. My mind is made up. As soon as
Georgina returns, I shall ask her to drive me to
Bradburn. I don't know how the trains run, but I
really think I shall get on the first one I see with its
buffers pointing south.

Detective-Superintendent Grimshaw came out to
Hempshaw End to take personal charge of the search-
party. The amount of uniformed help allocated to him
was even less than the Assistant Chief Constable had
promised. The lecturer in charge of the Technical College group looked as if he had been up half the night
trying to do justice to a particularly demanding seraglio.
And three quarters of his students looked as if one more
erotic encounter would be the death of them. One
couple in particular struck him. The boy was making
constant whispered appeals to the girl from the corner
of his mouth, and it was obvious that her answers were
affording him little satisfaction. Several times she tried
to sidle away from him and tack herself on to the main
body. When they started allocating squads for the work
ahead, she quite deftly managed to get herself parted
from her would-be escort at last. But Grimshaw, a
soured impishness in him this morning, stepped in to
reorganize and put them together again.

Then he saw the teacher in charge of the Junior
School bearing down on him with a merry cohort of
potential corpse-hunters. Grimshaw knew, of course,
that that would not do. Technical College students were
permissible. Small boys with unbroken voices and little
girls with their hair in pony-tails were not. He could
foresee the national press, the television cameras, the
country up in arms against the cynical callousness of its
law-enforcers. He could hear in his brain every syllable of the one-sided interview that would take place in
the Assistant Chief Constable's office.

"I'm sorry," he said to the teacher in charge, who had an Afro hairstyle and a gold (or brass) ring in one ear.

"It's good of you to offer to help. But, you know, it wouldn't be suitable. The sights that we are likely to come on—"

"We don't try to shield them from the realities of life these days," the teacher said.

"This might be the reality of death."

"All the better."

"I beg your pardon?"

"Last month we took them to a stud farm. They really *did* see action."

"I hope it will come in useful to them in due course. But this would hardly be the thing. Besides—it's difficult country, could be dangerous. Bogs. Fast-flowing streams. Crumbling cliffs."

"Whack-oh! Some of them are looking forward to coming to grips with the Duke's Award."

Grimshaw thought of the paucity of his line abreast, and he weakened. Rationalizing, he thought he saw a way.

"All right, then—I'll use you strictly as a reserve—a sort of line of whippers-in. The adults and the college students will be first over the ground, but there's no telling what they might miss. It would be a great credit to your children, if they were to pick up something that's been overlooked."

A sergeant came up and reported that the flanks of the task force were in position. Detective-Superintendent Grimshaw drew a whistle from his pocket and self-consciously blew it.

According to all the studies of the sexual drive that Nigel had read, this trauma ought to have had her clinging to him for orgiastic relief. Was not procreation the natural human response to death and destruction? Were not the slopes of volcanoes classically strewn with

copulating couples who ought more rationally to have
been fleeing for their lives? But there seemed to be
something about Sue that was not according to the
book. Far from tearing off her clothes and snatching at
the zip of his fly, she seemed to have been sapped of
all her urges. There seemed scarcely anything feminine
about her any more. Her hair could have been a man's.
Nigel looked at the barely disturbed contours under the
jacket-pockets of her denim jacket and wondered
whether she actually had breasts or not.

When they had first looked into the plate-layer's
hut, she had readily agreed with him about keeping
their mouths shut. But since then she had given what
Nigel considered a demonstration of femininity. She
had started saying that they ought to report what they
had seen, and from there it had not taken her long to
become obsessed with the idea. In vain did Nigel remind her that they had broken into the place, and that
that would be the first thing to interest the authorities.

"*You* broke into it," Sue said, dissociating herself
with the facility of Eve.

"And you were with me. You wanted to go in there.
And you've not forgotten why."

"Well, thank God we didn't," she said.

"I don't know why you say that."

"Because," she said, with logical finality.

But Nigel had not quite given up yet. He was a trier.
He tramped solidly beside her, his shoulder bumping
against hers. She actually tried to quicken her stride.

It so happened, because of their place in the line,
that their axis of advance took them along the edge of
the cutting that overlooked the Old Railway. It was
another group—a knot of villagers, including two
women—who were advancing up the track itself. Sue
and Nigel caught sight of them when they were about
fifteen yards short of the old cabin.

"Well—it'll all be over bar the shouting in a minute,"
Nigel said. "Then you'll be wondering what the hell
you've been worrying about all this time."

They stopped to watch what would happen. The group was moving slowly, two of the men halfway up the banks of the cutting, beating at thick tussocks of grass with sticks. One of the women went up to the door of the gangers' hut and put her hand on the handle. The door opened easily for her.

"Hey! It isn't locked," Nigel said.

The woman started to go into the hut and they waited for her to scream. But all she did was insert her torso, look casually round inside, then come out shrugging her shoulders.

"Somebody must have taken that padlock away," Nigel said.

Sue put her hands on the wall and shouted down into the cutting.

"What's in there?"

"Nothing," the woman shouted back. "Except two empty beer cans and about forty thousand spiders."

"Do keep up with the line, you two," said Grimshaw's voice from behind them.

No one who knew Sammy Bagshaw—no one even who loved him (if anyone did)—would have put his name forward for an exercise that demanded concentration, discipline, staying-power and at least some degree of knowledge of what was going on. At the age of eight, Sammy Bagshaw had not yet developed to the stage of thoroughly understanding all that was happening about him. There were even some forecasters who maintained that he never would. It took the sang-froid of the teacher with the Afro hairstyle and a ring in one ear to include Sammy in a field-studies expedition that was to live for a week away from home. Warned by his headmaster of what he was taking on, this teacher had simply remarked that just because a laddie had an IQ of sixty-five that was no reason why he should be socially deprived.

It might be interesting to attempt a Sammy Bagshaw's

eye view of all that happened to him that day, but it would be difficult to say with any exactitude what was his impression of events at any given time. He must, for example, have known what his breakfast was, for he ate it. He must have known that it was raining, for social involvement was not his only area of deprivation, and he did not possess a coat.

Presumably he thought that their movement in line up the rising flank of the moors was some sort of game, for he enquired who had the ball.

It is not impossible, in normal circumstances, for a boy to get lost, but it is improbable that he will do so when moving across open country with a companion only a yard or two away from him on either side, a teacher a few paces behind, and a police constable keeping an eye on the sector. Nevertheless, Sammy did get lost, and he added to the magnitude of this feat by managing also to penetrate the line of keenly observant adults in front of him, without being observed by any of them. He was certainly himself unable to account for his being where he eventually was—but then, he could rarely do that at the best of times.

What mattered was that Sammy Bagshaw, having got himself ahead of the main body, was the first to make a find. What he found was a woman's coat, hanging on the branches of a budding hawthorn that was apparently able to draw enough sustenance to live in a crack in a patch of exposed rock face. It was, as Sammy was later heard to describe it, a *funny* coat. It had grey fur on its reversed collar and a yoke of grey fur round its middle. It was much longer than any coat that Sammy had ever seen on a woman.

Sammy was not surprised by his find. If surprise had been a regular reaction in Sammy's existence, he would surely have gone about with permanently raised eyebrows, since in a world governed by no analysable pattern of reason, practically everything must surely be to some extent astonishing. Nor was Sammy entirely the fool that some people took him for. It was raining

hard, he was soaked to the skin, and he had just found a
coat. Insouciant of the figure that he cut—Janie Goodwin was a significantly taller person than he was—he
put it on.

Not every member of Detective-Superintendent Grimshaw's irregular army applied himself with equal dili-
gence and self-sacrifice to the objectives of the day.
Among those whose consciences could lightly be stilled
in this respect was Anthony Brakeshaft, the lecturer in
charge of the Technical College party. Having put his
forces at the disposal of the state—with the additional
bonus of having got them off his own hands for the
day—he saw no reason to indulge in what looked as if it
was going to be a twenty-mile tramp, to judge from
the marked map that that bloody policeman was carrying. The rain was by now fair pissing down, and he saw
no sense either in getting wetter than he already was.
Time would be far better spent rising to the challenge
of seduction—an art in which Tony Brakeshaft was more
accomplished, because more eclectically experienced,
than was Nigel Teesdale. Furthermore, his target was
distinctly less uninformed on procedural matters than
was Sue Grayson. In fact, the word "seduction" crossed
his mind only out of courtesy to the lady.

Brakeshaft had not really noticd Penny Evans until
last night. He had noticed her while leaning over her to
show his interest in a routine calculation that appeared
to be puzzling her. He was leaning at such an angle,
and she turned to look up at him through such an arc
that her columns of figures were not all that he saw.

"Your log tan angle of elevation can't possibly be
right," he said, maintaining the pressure on her shoulder that he had put there only tentatively in the first
instance. She agreed with the most skilful of smiles and
did nothing to suggest that she wanted the pressure
removed.

"I seem to have got into the habit recently of squinting down the wrong column."

She was dark-haired, looked after her hair more formally than most of her contemporaries did, was well made, tending to be stocky rather than chubby. She was highly practised in a smile that melted most men whom she wanted to melt, and she was quite clearly not indisposed to melt Anthony Brakeshaft at this juncture in a week in the country. She was also adept at conveying messages. The message now in transit was that she was well acquainted with her own equipment, that she knew what it was for and how to use it to advantage. And that if Mr. Brakeshaft was interested, that suited her.

But unfortunately she shared a bedroom at the Centre with a girl who was an unknown quantity to Brakeshaft, and whom he saw at the moment no tactical way of dislodging. He was disinclined, however, to let the encounter remain as brief as that.

Now, this morning, Penny Evans was not looking her happiest in a light plastic raincoat, at the end of a line that had just started across yet another field. It had to be admitted, on the other hand, that the raincoat did something for her. It seemed to accentuate a very healthy mobility.

It had also to be admitted that the line discipline was not very good on this sector of the front. There were other members of the college besides their moral tutor whose hearts were not totally committed to what they had volunteered for. And one or two had already succeeded in slipping out of the line altogether, which accounted for gaps in it and its state of general raggedness.

On the pretext of closing ranks, Brakeshaft went over to within earshot of Penny. "Not too good a morning, Miss Evans."

"I can think of places where I'd rather be."

"For example?"

"Somewhere warm, dry and unfrequented."

A few minutes later they found what filled the bill, a group of sheds on a farm that seemed completely deserted. Maybe the inhabitants were all out in the line somewhere.

Brakeshaft shouted over to the man nearest on his left that he was going to give these possible hidey-holes the once-over. The rest of them were to keep the line tight, and he would catch up with them.

He passed behind Penny and beckoned her with a jerk of his head. They had to make their way round a slough where cattle had passed. She looked at him with a grin that anticipated something unsentimental, but of undoubted technical accomplishment. He pushed open one or two sheds, rejecting them as dirty or occupied by creatures unconducive to pure romance. Then he found one that was roomier than the others, and that had recently had space cleared in it.

To some purpose: in one corner an executioner's scaffold had been erected, on which stood a toothy-grinned effigy made from old sacks, strapped, noosed and waiting its hour on the drop. There was nothing scarey about it. Even at a distance and in that poorish light, one could see at once that it was only a scarecrow.

Brakeshaft went up to the lever and pulled it hard over. The trap fell with a creak and a clatter, and the effigy, still grinning, fell swinging into the depths.

Not all of Grimshaw's mobile brigade were backsliders. The Hemp Valley had volunteered in some strength, and there were men and women who worked with dedication in spite of the weather, poking sticks into any vegetation that was at all dense, stirring up leaf-mould, examining dung-heaps for signs of recent turning, getting down on their hands and knees in wet grass to look into ditches and under hedgerows. The first find to go into the official log was discovered stuffed behind a loose stone beside a stile. It was a lady's camisole in a kind of muslin trimmed with imitation lace, and was of

a pattern much favoured during the reign of Edward
VII.

Halfway through the morning, Detective-Superintendent Grimshaw called a halt to take stock of general
progress and to redeploy his troops in places where
multiple desertions had left serious inadequacies in his
striking power. A fair amount of woman's underclothing
had now been brought in, all of it dating from the first
decade of the century, but all of it still in excellent
condition. He reported to the Assistant Chief Constable
over the radio network that there appeared to be an
element of the ridiculous about the exercise.

"The stuff is spread over such a wide area: a left
elastic-sided boot a mile and a half from its neighbour,
a pair of black ankle-length riding drawers some seven
hundred yards from a high-necked, half-sleeved pure
silk vest. Moreover, this is not a subject on which I
would profess personal expertise, but I *am* a married
man, and it does seem to me that none of this stuff has
been recently worn. What I mean is, not to put too fine
a point on it—it doesn't seem to me to have just come
off a lady's back."

Then, short-breathed from a mixture of excitement
and exertion, a man came running into the mobile
headquarters to report the discovery of a gallows in
good working order.

And so the day came to an end at last. Grimshaw had
had enough of it.

There had been all that lingerie. Grimshaw had pinned
flags all over his map, showing where vests, knickers,
chemises and combinations had been found. He was
beginning to suspect that this thing might possibly be a
hoax; then the inspiration came to him that there might
be some sort of significant pattern in the distribution of
the garments. It might be somebody's way of trying to
tell him something. He plotted the finds accordingly,
and the design he produced looked now like the left-
hand profile of an eagle, now like the tail-feathers of a

duck facing right. The thought kept coming to him—he told himself unjustly—that Mosley was behind this somewhere—and he, who had suffered deeply and consistently from Mosley in the past, wondered what he had done to deserve this new wave of venom. For although in the past Mosley had sometimes been obstinate, sometimes stupid, often devious and occasionally able to prove himself right in the end, he had never before shown himself as implacably bloody-minded as this.

It was not only a matter of Janie Goodwin's eccentric underwear. The day had also been overshadowed by those bloody gallows. The FOR SALE advertisement had been brought up in the first instance by the Assistant Chief Constable. Beamish had come back from Mosley with the tale of Billy Birkin. Then, towards the end of the morning, a man had come up panting to announce that he had found the contraption. Well and good. But within five minutes another Mercury had arrived also panting, and declaring the whereabouts of a second engine of death. It was not more than an hour and a half before a third was placed on record. By the end of the working day—that is, by the first failure of daylight—Grimshaw had been to see with his own eyes six working sets of gallows: one in a shed behind a widow's cottage; two on farm complexes, three on various smallholdings dotted up and down the Valley. He still had not got to hear about the one in the platelayer's hut that had disturbed the promising relationship between Nigel Teesdale and Sue Grayson; and that had appeared to be missing when the search-party passed that way this morning.

So what was it about the Hemp Valley that made it the thing of the moment to possess the means of formal extermination? The initial statements of the owners had been somehow unconvincing.

"Just curiosity, I suppose," one of them said.

"I always have been interested in that sort of thing," came from another.

"I thought that if we ever had a break-in and a burglar saw it on the premises, he might have second thoughts."

"We were going to give Sunday-morning shows. In aid of the Church of England Children's Society."

Subject to the smaller print in manuals of police law that he had not yet had the chance to consult, Grimshaw did not think that the possession of a scaffold, however efficiently maintained, was in itself an offence. And when all was said and done, there were other things higher up in his mind than the fashion for gallows.

There had been, for example, two more disappearances, one of which, he knew, was going to be attended by more denigratory publicity than anything else that had ever happened in his career. For he had just been on the point of dismissing his troops and driving back to Bradburn for a cup of sweet tea and a leisurely glance through anything else that had come in today, when it was reported to him in panic that one of the children from the Junior School was missing.

Not that little moron Sammy Bagshaw. Sammy had not even been reported missing. He had returned to his unit before anyone had missed him, with the hem of Janie Goodwin's coat trailing on the ground and the cuffs turned up nearly to his elbows. He had cried bitterly when they had taken the coat off him, but otherwise had been unable to give any account of himself. He could not state articulately where he had found the coat. Even the most subtle probing had not elicited where he had been. The information that he had succeeded in coaxing out of Sammy Bagshaw had to be counted among Grimshaw's professional failures.

There had been a letter in Janie Goodwin's coatpocket, a letter addressed to Janie Goodwin and folded back into the envelope in which it had originally been posted. It was a cryptic letter. Grimshaw had not so far managed to make head or tail of it. For just as he was making his third attempt to read it, six overexcited

little girls had come running up ahead of their teacher
to let it be known that Brenda Shuttleworth was not to
be found.

It took a good deal of piecing together, and Grimshaw
was by no means convinced that he had succeeded in
piecing it together correctly. It seemed that the contingent of which Brenda was a popular member had stopped
to eat their packed lunch in the grounds of a sawmill,
when Brenda had said that she was going over into the
next field to exchange reminiscences with some of the
Second Year. When she did not return, it was taken for
granted that she had tacked herself on to the Second
Year for the remainder of the day's sport. No one in the
Second Year, however, had seen anything of Brenda
Shuttleworth at all. Grimshaw sent two of his uniformed minions off to the sawmill in the failing light
and said that he would follow in a few minutes' time.

But this he was unable to do; he had just radioed this
latest set-back to the Bradburn office when he saw
that the retired schoolmistress, Miss Crane, was ap-
proaching. He had hitherto docketed her in his mind as
a woman of some aplomb, but today something seemed
to have shaken her. There was a greyness about her
features and she was having difficulty in keeping her
fingers still.

Miss Elizabeth Stirrup, her young friend and former
pupil, had, it seemed, vanished into the rain-swept
air. Miss Crane had left her alone in the house while
she went down into the village to organize haversack
rations for the search-party, and when she got back, it
looked as if Miss Stirrup had been making preparations
for unexpected departure. Her suitcase was packed, but
was still standing on a chair with the lid open. Her
diary was also lying open on a table and her last sen-
tence had been left unfinished.

"She's a young lady who's capable of looking after
herself, I would imagine," Grimshaw said hopefully.

"I would not be so sure of that. I have taken the
liberty of peeping into the pages of that diary, and I am

greatly perturbed by the way she seems to have developed. Or should I say, not developed?"

The next unavoidable hazard was a confrontation with the ACC. The latest entries in the log would not properly have sunk into the ACC's mind yet, and it might well be some time before they did. He was not a man capable of undertaking very many simultaneous mental processes: two was about the limit—and even that was exceptional.

Nor was he a man on whose desk information was quick to arrive, and when it did, he did not always grasp its true significance at once—or even, as a rule, after repetitive explanation. Today, however, he seemed to have been in the toils of an intellectual blizzard. He was positively exploding with information. A report from Forensic had apparently landed in front of him while his Detective-Superintendent was out in the field, and not only had he understood it, his mind had pounced on its main implications. The blood on the reed matting from Janie Goodwin's kitchen, like that on the Guinness bottle with which it had been presumed that she had had her head bashed in, had been firmly identified as that of a rabbit. And the wisp of hair adhering to it had, it seemed, been detached from a sheep.

"One is tempted to think," the Assistant Chief Constable said, "that someone set out deliberately to make it look as if this woman had been attacked."

Grimshaw then filled him in on the day's other unsatisfactory stories: the scattering of Janie Goodwin's intimate effects over a generous area; the proliferation of hangman's apparatus; the misadventure of Sammy Bagshaw; the loss of Brenda Shuttleworth; the spiriting away of Elizabeth Stirrup.

"This is becoming a serious business," the ACC said, then tapped Forensic's report. "If only you'd known about this earlier, you could have been looking for a discarded rabbit-skin while you were about it."

"Or for a sheep with a wisp of wool missing?" Grimshaw asked between his teeth.

"But the rabbit that the blood came from could surely be an important piece of primary evidence, could it not? I always think that—"

But then the Assistant Chief Constable pulled off the day's treble. Something else occurred to him. "It's a pity you had to employ children to look for a cadaver," he said.

Grimshaw went back to the sweet silence of his own office, reached for a sheet of paper and began to write a mnemonic list of the things that he ought to be doing. He had not gone further than the second line when someone came to his door. It was Sergeant Beamish.

"You told me to report to you personally at the end of the day, sir. I have been with Mosley since early this morning. I'm afraid I'm not entirely clear in my mind about what's going on, sir."

11

Beamish's briefing by Mosley had been to report early on the Saturday at Barker's Clough to put up the Widow Rawlings's curtains for her. Something had also been said in a casual fashion about perhaps ironing them for her while he was about it. But Beamish told himself that this had probably not registered properly on Mrs. Rawlings's mind, and that she probably would not want it, anyway.

He wondered what hour counted as early in Barker's Clough. Some of these old daleswomen had probably broken the back of their housework by sun-up. He decided to compromise. He would get there early, but not make any close approach until he was certain that there was life about the place. Dawn that day, such as it was, was scheduled to break round about half-past six. It was not so much a spreading of light as a preliminary notice of the rain that had not yet started. Beamish drove into Barker's Clough and parked his car in a spot from which he could see the windows of the house without getting dangerously close. The first thing that violently struck him was that the curtains were already back in place. They had not been drawn to but hung neatly and motionlessly where they belonged. "Motionlessly" was the appropriate word, for there was nothing about the house to suggest that it was inhabited—not a flutter of wing or fur in the yard, not a showing of smoke from a chimney. Well—that need not have much significance. Mrs. Rawlings had given the impression yesterday of being one of those dour old women who keep themselves in trim by wishing privation on themselves. She probably did not light a fire until her morning chores were behind her, preferring to enliven her circulation by the activity of her limbs.

Then Beamish did see a token signal from a cowl— not a vigorous plume, but a thin rising spiral, as from a cigarette that a man is forgetting to smoke. He decided to go up and make himself known, though he did not now see what he could usefully achieve. As the curtains were already up, the reason for his visit had been pre-empted. Had Mrs. Rawlings been physically capable of rehanging them without assistance? It was hardly likely that the sight of him would bring her pleasure. She would merely assume that this was a second unwanted invasion of her domestic privacy.

He drew up in the yard, parked his car with its bonnet pointing for a dignified getaway should he run into a hurricane of abuse. Again he had the forceful impression that the house was unoccupied: no face behind the curtains, no cat on the sill, not even a bird

waiting for an expected crumb. Even the windows had
that lifeless look that can only be managed by glass that
finds nothing worth reflecting; the sky was a uniform
deep grey. The rain would not hold off much longer.

He put his hand to the latch and to his surprise it
lifted readily. He stepped into the living-room in which
he had talked to Mosley and the widow yesterday. It
was in every respect a cold room. The stone walls
enclosed a temperature that felt chillier than the air
outside. The grate, in which a cheerful coal fire had
been burning yesterday, had been thoroughly cleaned
out. A small quantity of paper, three or four sheets
from a cheap correspondence pad, had been recently
burned. There was still slight warmth in the ashes as
Beamish touched them lightly with his knuckles. Perhaps this accounted for the vestigial smoke that he had
seen from a distance.

"Mrs. Rawlings!"

He called her name, but there was no response.
There sounded something ineffectual in his voice, which
seemed to carry nowhere. He remembered that she
was very deaf.

He was now convinced that he was on the brink of
coming upon some sight for which he had better steel
himself. He pushed open a door that he had not seen
opened yesterday. The house, though not large, was
asymmetrically complex. He found himself in a dark
and narrow stone-flagged passage that wandered round
right-angles between the doors of rooms that had previously performed some function in the No Man's Land
between farming and housekeeping. He opened and
shut them, saw a jumble of old zinc baths, of vats,
churns and troughs. It must have been months or years
since anyone had been in to look at this junk.

He thought he heard a single footfall behind him, as
if someone else had come out of the kitchen, but when
he spun on his heel and dashed back, there was no one
there. Then he thought he heard the opening and shut-

ting of a door, and the crunch of a foot on the ground outside. He rushed to the window, having to knock over obstacles to get there. But he could see no one—though suddenly he caught sight of his own car. Nonsensically, there seemed something unexpected in seeing it there.

"Mrs. Rawlings!"

There came back only emptiness. He went upstairs, observed that only one bedroom was in regular use. All the others were cold, dusty, and repositories for unwanted furniture. The widow's room was what he might have expected of it—a chair, a commode, a chest of drawers from the turn of the century, a text on the wall, a general eschewing of colour or comfort.

He went down and out of the house to look round its surrounds. There were several sheds and outhouses, all of them cluttered with bygones. In one he saw a neat stack of timber, cut in varying lengths, and with numbers painted on the components, as if to assist assembly. There were corner stanchions, handrails and a rudimentary lever resembling those used by railway signalmen. Surely Mrs. Rawlings had not done a deal for Billy Birkin's abortive vocational equipment? And all the time that he was looking, he seemed to keep hearing single footsteps, now round this corner, now round that, now to his left, now to his right, but always behind him, usually obliquely so, and always proving him mistaken when he kept moving round walls and angles to make sure.

He made another systematic tour inside and outside the house before deciding that there was definitely no one to be found, then got into his car and started the engine. There was only one next move to make in such a situation as this, and that was to refer it to Mosley. He had taken no risks, had made written notes of the catalogue of Neighbouring that Mosley had had in mind for the day. This morning, if Beamish was not mistaken, he had intended to call on an elderly man in a village called Hadley Dale and give him a lesson in riding a bicycle. The first drops of rain began hitting Beamish's windscreen as he drove back down through Barker's Clough. Conditions were not going to be ideal for outdoor pursuits.

To reach Hadley Dale, a village some fifteen miles away and situated in a different valley, he had to pass through Hempshaw End. Grimshaw's miscellaneous squad was just waiting to form up as Beamish approached. He saw the Junior School, all eager to stumble over decomposing corpses in marshy hollows. Had Grimshaw the vaguest idea what he might be stirring up here? Beamish saw Nigel and Sue, the girl trying to side-step away from her companion, as a pigeon on a railway platform may be seen declining the advances of a cock who has got his timing wrong. He caught sight of Grimshaw, who at that moment was holding his whistle in his hand, swinging it to and fro at the end of a short lanyard. And the sight of Grimshaw caused his feet to go to his clutch and brake pedals simultaneously. He reversed into a field entrance and drove back some way along the road by which he had come. Because he knew that if Grimshaw saw him, he might easily have second thoughts about his spending the working day with Mosley.

When Beamish returned through Hempshaw End, Grimshaw's command had advanced from its start-line, so he was able to make his way through the village unimpeded. Beamish did not think he had ever seen a human settlement so quiet in the daytime. The streets were deserted. No one was coming or going from the shops. Except for the odd house-bound paralytic, everyone in the place must be out getting merrily soaked. Beamish's route took him up past the schoolhouse, and there at last he did see someone.

Coming down from the old school towards the village, he saw a man and woman walking very close together. The woman he recognized at once as Miss Stirrup, Miss Crane's young friend, of whom he retained the most neutral of impressions. He waved to her, and she looked at him with the most neutral of expressions, as if she was not sure whether the wave was meant for her or not, but she would certainly have resented it if it were. As he was driving past at about thirty-three miles an hour, Beamish did not exactly take a mental photograph of the man. He was therefore not able to give a very full description when that later became desirable. But he saw that he was a man past his prime, hatless and wearing a camel-hair coat that must have cost him several months' earnings of a detective-sergeant.

It took Beamish about half an hour to reach Hadley Dale. It was a village with a nucleus, for the main street broadened out in front of its post office and two pubs and would have made a suitable arena for an annual fair, if one had ever been held. It was not to be expected that there would be many people about this morning, for the rain was now lashing across this public place in a horizontal sheet. But even at that, the village looked no more occupied than Hempshaw End had done. The lifelessness had something frighteningly unnatural about it—a sort of community catalepsy. There ought, Beamish thought, to be *somebody* abroad. There must surely be some piece of gossip that demanded transmission, come hell or high water, some packet of salt or can of beans to be acquired for hard cash. But the two pubs—not famous for their recognition of licensing hours—looked as quiescent as the churchyard. A bread van was standing outside one cottage. Its rear doors were swinging open, and the fury of the storm was whipping in on the wrapped, sliced loaves. But no baker's vanman was in evidence.

Then Beamish did see someone: a small child running vigorously the length of the broad street, up to the ankles in every puddle that stood in his way.

Beamish wound down his window. "Where," he shouted, "is everyone?"

"Mr. Mosley is teaching old Steve to ride a bike. Everybody's gone to watch. It's going to be good."

The boy, who had hardly stopped running to answer, was already disappearing at the far end of the street. Beamish cruised slowly forward, in time to see him dodge through the gateway of the village hall.

And in that building, some couple of hundred people were standing tightly packed against the walls, watching an old man of short stature ride round the cleared wooden floor-space in long ellipses, careful not to allow the soles of both feet to leave the ground at the same time. Standing at the geometrical centre of these gyrations, his raincoat open, his black hat safely jammed into place, Mosley looked like a classical circus ringmaster. He was extremely pleased to see Beamish.

"Ah! The very man! Take over from me, will you? Something else has blown up. I've got to go and attend to it."

The rider was at that moment disentangling himself from a minor spill. As Beamish was helping him to his feet and holding the machine for him to remount, he heard the uniquely identifiable racket of Mosley's car-engine starting up outside.

Even as it was passing, Beamish knew that the next half-hour was going to rank as one of the unhappiest he had ever spent. He was no more cut out for giving cycling instruction than Steve Blamire was for receiving it. Blamire was not even properly dressed for the activity. His trousers had been bought off their original peg by a much taller man, and even clips, if he had been wearing them, would not have kept their turn-ups from enveloping the pedals. And Beamish's material teaching problems caused him to overlook the proper disciplinary command of his audience. In their excitement, they had begun to advance from the positions tight against the wall in which Mosley had fixed them. Some of the children, their interest in the spectacle flagging, had begun to encroach, to their peril, on the

Lebensraum that Old Steve needed. And Old Steve, angry and surprised at his repeated failures in public, turned his wrath against the shortcomings of his instructor, which was just what the public was waiting for. They missed Mosley—and began to hiss Beamish.

He was saved by the arrival of an extremely crusty old sexton, who also served as caretaker of the Hall. It seemed that Mosley had taken the building for this nefarious purpose without proper consultation; but it was Beamish who was clearly going to take the entire blame.

He was not inclined to defend himself. He was only too happy to see an end of this lunatic activity. Then the crowd bunched up in the doorway, and it was impossible to exit with any kind of dignity.

But before Beamish could push his way back to his car, he felt his sleeve being pulled. It was the sexton again, now winking in a manner that Beamish thought at first was a facial tic.

"Excuse me, sir. Mr. Mosley asked me to break the proceedings up. He would like you to call at Mrs. Foley's. He is tuning her piano."

"Tuning her piano?"

"That's what he said, sir."

Mrs. Foley's cottage was a snug little cube that might have figured as an illustration in a sentimental history of the English home. It had a great deal in it that was of sentimental interest—including a fifty-year-old radio receiver that still worked with valves and an accumulator. But Beamish was in no mood to be moved by sentimental evocation. The morning had rattled him. He had had enough. In particular, he had had enough of Mosley. It was no mere question of umbilical parting— the cord was in imminent danger of actual explosion. His bile was not relieved by the sight of Mosley himself, looking incredibly more foolish than in any man's worst imaginings. Mosley had taken off his coat, and had pushed his hat back towards the back of his head.

"I'll go and get you a cuppa."

Mrs. Foley left the room, and Beamish advanced truculently on Mosley. "What the hell are you up to now, you damed old idiot? You know you don't know how to tune a bloody piano."

"I shall know more about it, by the time I've done with this one."

He had taken the front off the ancient rosewood upright, and at least seemed to have equipped himself with the right kind of keys and hammers.

"After all, I've seen it done. I can sing in tune. I know what a scale is. It's only a matter of tightening up a length of wire here, slackening one off a shade there. You don't happen to have a tuning fork on you, do you?"

"I'm sorry. I left it in my other suit."

Beamish had had no idea that the inside of a musical instrument could smell as revolting as this one did. There was historic dust within this article of furniture. Its ledges, cracks and crevices were spilling over with what moths had done with the felt of its dampers and hammers. Mosley gave his key a little knock to get it to turn a specially recalcitrant peg. This set up a sympathetic twanging from deep down in the frame of the thing.

Mrs. Foley came back with Beamish's tea. She looked at the pair of them with lachrymose admiration. "It must be wonderful to be able to turn your hand to anything," she said.

"It would be, wouldn't it?" Beamish said, when she had gone again.

"Don't be cynical, Beamish. It's all in a good cause."

"You also belong to a club for the destruction of your neighbours' pianos, I take it?"

"I am very anxious to impress Mrs. Foley."

"Oh. I thought you were trying to provoke her to bring a civil action against you."

"There is certain information that I want her to pass on to us voluntarily. She has a seven-year-old grand-daughter coming to stay with her next week—a child who has taken the first rung of the ladder, and is entering for an elementary examination of the Royal College of Music. It is essential that this instrument should be in tip-top condition for her to practise on."

Mosley played by ear the first few bars of "Abide with Me" and listened critically to the echo.

"And, you know, piano-tuning is damned pricey these days. A professional job, I mean."

He knocked the peg through another few degrees. A string of the B flat below middle C snapped with a crack like a starting-pistol.

"Bloody hell!" Mosley said.

"Actually, I do have another pressing engagement this morning, Mr. Mosley."

"You'd do better to stick with me, laddie. You're going to learn something. Mrs. Foley was the wife of a man who was a gardener at Hempshaw Hall in the time of the Goodwins. She knows a thing or two that the Fraud Squad would have given their ears to find out about at one time."

Mosley was silent for at least a minute and appeared to be applying his best attention to the piano. But Beamish noticed that his plan of attack had changed. He was making a lot of noise, occasionally testing it with very simple tunes (he really was a pretty awful pianist) and actually doing very little to the strings. Maybe he had taken fright at the single wire that had snapped so far, and his main effort now was going in to making Mrs. Foley think that he really was tuning the thing. Did he so badly want to ingratiate himself with her?

"Do you know," Mosley said, "that when John Foley came into a small family legacy in the late 1940s—it was about £400—Wilson Goodwin got to know about it and actually borrowed £250 from him?"

"And did he ever get it back?"

"That is one of the things that I aim to find out from Mrs. Foley."

Mosley played a few bars of "The Bluebells of Scot-

land," following it up with a badly executed chromatic
scale down three and a half octaves.

"I'm pretty sure he got at least some of it back. What
interests me is the circumstances in which it came to be
repaid. Was Wilson Goodwin suddenly affluent?"

"Home, Sweet Home"—did Mosley know how to
play anything that wasn't in the first "Tutor" that he
had had as a child? There was something slightly revolting in the thought of Mosley as a child.

"I went to hang Mrs. Rawlings's curtains as you told
me to," Beamish said.

"Oh, aye?"

"They were already hung."

"I hoped they might be."

Mosley executed a scale in octaves in the key of C
major.

"And Mrs. Rawlings was not there."

"Good. They got her away in good time, then."

"Got her away?"

Mosley made some impressively technical adjustment
to one of the dampers. A large pinch of moth-eaten
felt came away under his thumb.

"Mr. Mosley—are you listening to me?"

Mosley stopped what he was doing, stretched his
fingers over the keyboard and turned to look at Beamish, all attention.

"Something very peculiar indeed was going on at
Barker's Clough," Beamish said. "I got the feeling that
I was not alone in the place. Somebody had been
burning paper in the grate just before I went into the
house. I heard footsteps inside and out, but whoever it
was was able to vanish round corners. It's a maze of a
place, an absolute gift to anybody trying to hide from
one man. Mr. Mosley—what's going on?"

"It'll all come out in the wash."

"Is that all you're prepared to tell me?"

Mosley tinkled a few more notes, as a cover for a
moment's thinking.

"*You* know what's going on. Aren't you going to put me in the picture?"

"I'd rather you didn't put that sort of pressure on me," Mosley said.

"But I have my position to consider."

"That thought is uppermost in my mind."

"I don't mean that I'm spying on behalf of Grimshaw—though I'm supposed to be. But I'm not all that keen on undermining what chances I have in the force."

"Quite rightly. I'd hate you to think that I'm doing anything unprofessional."

"I wouldn't for a moment."

This, Beamish reflected, was hypocrisy superbly refined: Mosley looking up from the keyboard of an instrument that he hadn't a clue how to deal with; himself pretending a naïve confidence in the man's innocence.

"Just as long as it's nothing illegal—" Beamish said.

"I'm doing nothing illegal. In fact, I'm doing practically nothing at all. A natural process is taking place, Sergeant Beamish. An issue that needed justice is about to be justly resolved. And by justice I don't mean wigs, gowns and the Law Society taxing solicitors' dishonest accounts. Nor am I taking any active part in this process. I'm what the chemists would call a catalyst. I speed up reactions without taking part in them. What I'm doing is in no way unprofessional—but I can quite see that a mind as narrow as Grimshaw's might find it so."

He played the opening strain of "Won't You Buy My Pretty Flowers?"

"And it's not only justice that I can see being served. There is such a thing as self-fulfilment. As a rule, there is little that an outsider can do about that. But it has to be noted too that there are times when self-fulfilment would never happen without outside influence."

"You know you can rely on me to be with you in anything like that."

Mosley did a five-finger exercise at the lower end of the keyboard.

"I know that. That's the only reason you are here this morning, helping me to do this. But what you don't *know*, you can't be called to account for."

"We went over all this once before."

"That was only over a simple case of burglary. There are jacks-in-office who would get terribly hot under the collar over present events as I see them."

"Have it your own way. I've just remembered something else." It was remarkable, Beamish thought, how ordinary mental processes seemed to break down when Mosley was about. "The Widow Rawlings had a neatly stacked gallows in one of her sheds."

"That I didn't know."

Nor did he seem particularly moved by the intelligence. There were some old ladies who had their own gallows, there were some who didn't. It was a matter of basic indifference to Mosley.

"She can be a bit of a virago. I can see that," Beamish said, "but I can't quite see her topping anybody single-handed."

"I dare say she never will."

Mosley was becoming more and more laconic as the piano absorbed him.

"I can understand Grimshaw feeling uneasy at having these things up and down the county."

"Any number of people have been getting on the bandwagon," Mosley said. "It's only to be expected."

"Bandwagon?"

Mosley stopped work for the sake of making a definite statement. "It's just like our head office, isn't it? It's three or four months since Billy Birkin put his apparatus on the market. A newspaper cutting gets stuck to a paper-clip in somebody's in-tray, and it's weeks before anyone picks it up. Then they want action at panic speed. The last thing I heard was that Billy was going to let it go to the women who wanted it for charity shows. That's just like Billy. He's no more head for business than he has for topping a dummy. He's made a word-of-mouth agreement with these women, and he regards that as binding. But it's anybody's guess what offers he's had from outsiders. I've heard about a few of them. Old Noll Cromwell made the thing for Billy's mother for a tenner. Now there's a holiday camp offering £500 for it to put it in a sideshow. At least two Third World countries want it for its original purpose. A waxworks on Bognor seafront wants it. The Castle Museum at York wants it. The BBC Drama Department want it as a stage property. And Billy Birkin isn't the man to keep all this to himself. Everybody's heard. So Noll Cromwell has gone into gallows-production on the grand scale. He's working overtime at his bench. Fifty quid, that's the inflated price, with an effigy thrown in as a free gift for cash payment. Everybody wants one as an investment."

"I see."

"Mind you, I'm not all that happy about it. You know what people are. When they've spent money on something, they start hankering to try it out."

"That's what Grimshaw feels."

"Well, I'm always happy to see Grimshaw occupied. It helps to keep him off my neck. But now you must let me get on with this. We can talk later. It isn't that Ma Foley is an uncooperative woman, she does suffer from a misplaced sense of loyalty: a very sentimental woman. She knows as well as anyone else—a damned sight more realistically than most—what sort of a turd Wilson Goodwin was. But her husband was employed on the estate, and she has an old-fashioned *esprit de corps*. But you wait till she sees what I've done with her joanna. I shall be on the receiving end of a very powerful sense of obligation."

So for the next hour he sat making what he judged to be the right range of sound-effects, interrupting the labour now and then for a short flight into melody: Handel's "March in Scipio" and even Beethoven's "Minuet in G." Then he got Beamish to help him put the front-board back into position, and he called in Mrs. Foley to witness the results of his handiwork. It was a very old waltz-song that he played for her, with a bold accompaniment of two thumped-out chords in the left hand.

> Bluebells I've gathered,
> Keep them and be true.
> When I'm a man,
> My plan
> Will be to marry you.

The corners of Mrs. Foley's eyes were moist. "Oh, you are a beautiful player. Mr. Mosley. Do you know, nobody's played a note on that piano since the war?"

12

Detective-Superintendent Grimshaw was distinctly despondent when Sergeant Beamish called on him as ordered at the end of the day. He looked grey. His eyes were as sagging and pathetic as a bloodhound's. His hands were resting limply on the desk in front of him, his wrists extending from his beautifully starched and linked cuffs. Between his hands lay the Churchillian single sheet of paper, on one side of which he had tried to marshal the tasks that were crowding in on him.

Seeing his master's dejection, Beamish felt that it behoved him to spread a little cheer and general optimism. Grimshaw looked at him as if another man's

smile was the last straw in his payload. He motioned
Beamish to sit down. Beamish did so, at the same time
doing his best to read Grimshaw's notes as well as he
could upside down. Grimshaw noted this, twisted the
paper round and slid it under Beamish's eyes.

(i) Brenda Shuttleworth
(ii) Elizabeth Stirrup
(iii) Underwear
(iv) Bloody rabbit
(v) Gallows
(vi) Jane Goodwin's letter

"Who," Beamish asked him, "is Brenda Shuttleworth?"
"She is nine years old. She was last seen wearing a
red and white knitted hat, and a red and white anorak
with sewn-on badges from Blackpool, Morecambe,
Southport, Scarborough, Whitby and Windermere. I
am sure she presents a striking picture, because she is
also wearing white slacks and red ankle-socks. Both
her upper eye-teeth are missing and so is she."
"Ah!"
"She is missing because a fool of a Detective-
Superintendent chose to employ a class of juveniles to
hunt for a corpse."
"I did wonder at the time about the wisdom of that,"
Beamish said, seldom the man to wrap up his opinions.
He was saved from petrification only because the
Detective-Superintendent chose not to acknowledge
the remark.
"I may say," Grimshaw said, "that though that is
what the press will undoubtedly say, it is not precisely
how it happened."
Beamish was silent.
"She went missing by a sawmill. Piper and Reynolds
are at that sawmill at the moment. You and I will join
them presently."
"And why is Elizabeth Stirrup's name on the list?"
"She's missing too."

"Ah!"

"Don't keep saying that, Sergeant Beamish. You don't advance matters by behaving as if you had inside information."

"In this case I think that I may have, sir."

Grimshaw looked at him as if he resented being teased with false hopes.

"I think that we are looking for a hatless man in late middle-age wearing a camel-hair coat."

Beamish remembered the couple walking down from the schoolhouse as he was driving out of Hempshaw End. He remembered how Elizabeth Stirrup had glowered at him when he had waved to her. He remembered how closely they had been walking together—unnaturally close, it now seemed to him—as close as a couple might be if one were holding a muzzle of a pistol against the other's ribs.

Grimshaw was looking at him not so much in amazement, as with the beginnings of anger. "What do you know, Sergeant Beamish? Kindly don't treat this as if it were some sort of charade."

"Sir—this is the first—"

"I know, I know, I know."

There was one thing about Grimshaw's unjust rages: they were always quick to subside.

"It is a pity you didn't stop to investigate."

"Sir—would you have done, do you honestly think?"

Grimshaw avoided the question. "You might as well go down the whole list while you're about it, Sergeant."

"Underwear," Beamish read aloud.

"There was a great deal of it, almost antique, and in first-class condition, scattered all over the landscape."

"Yes, sir. And what's this about a rabbit?"

"That's an obsession of the Assistant Chief Constable. You know what it's like when he's suffering from an idea."

Beamish did not, actually. In his present position in the force, he heard very little top office gossip.

"Until we close this file," Grimshaw said, "we are

going to be asked at frequent intervals whether we have found that bloody rabbit."

"I, of course, have yet to hear about the creature," Beamish said.

So Grimshaw told him what Forensic had had to say about the blood on the kitchen matting and the bottle.

"Ah, well, I can see the reason for that," Beamish said.

"You can, can you? Would you have any objection to sharing your theories with me, Sergeant?"

"Somebody wanted us to think she'd been killed, sir."

"Ah, yes—but who? I am sorry to nag you about trivialities, Sergeant . . ."

An answer had suddenly occurred to Beamish, remembering something that Mosley had said. The fish: Mosley had predicted that Grimshaw would be misled by the fish in the window. Mosley had made feeble jokes about it, because he had guessed—if not *known*—that Janie Goodwin had herself put that fish in her window—*after* she had wrecked her own room. An image had come into his mind of Mosley watching it happen: from Janie Goodwin's garden, where he had accidentally dropped his pipe.

"I think she did it herself, sir," Beamish said.

"There's no evidence for such a statement."

"There's the drawing of the fish, sir. Only she can have put it there. The intruder would hardly have drawn attention to his own handiwork, would he?"

"You may have a point there."

"Which suggests that Miss Goodwin—Mrs. Cromwell—wanted to make sure that it was not too long before the chaos was discovered."

Give Grimshaw his due: he was capable of imagination—especially when stimulated as Beamish was stimulating him.

"But she had no need to do that, had she? She knew that the Meals on Wheels would be coming."

"With respect, I think not, sir."

"Why not? It was Friday."

"Yes, sir—and the schools have already started their Easter holiday. She may not have known that the dinner was going to be cooked at the dye works. If you remember, Miss Crane told us that Cromwell didn't. He had already settled down to a plate of bread and butter when she called. Which suggests that the arrangement hadn't happened before."

"All right, Sergeant, I don't feel as certain about it as you do. But we'll bear the possibility in mind. Now what about all this unworn clothing all over the place?"

Grimshaw nodded at the wall-map on which he had plotted the finding of the garments. "I can't see any underlying pattern, can you, Beamish?"

"Yes, sir."

"And you propose to keep it to yourself?"

"Two things, I think, sir. First, the garments were picked up in the order in which they had been taken off."

"I think I should tell you that I have come to the firm conclusion, Sergeant, that they had never been on."

"Perhaps not, sir. So, let's say, in the order in which they would have been taken off."

"And why should anyone do that?"

"I come to my second point, sir. Someone was wanting to lead us in a certain direction—one must assume in the wrong direction."

"But if someone, whether Miss Goodwin herself or not, wanted us to think her dead, why not have a few gruesome touches about her lingerie?"

"I admit that that is a paradox."

"Not your most useful remark of the day."

"At one moment a bloody death is suggested. Then we get what may be a hint that she is unharmed."

"That doesn't make any kind of sense at all."

"Why not, sir? Suppose she had two people to impress. She wants one of them to think she has been killed. She wants to reassure the other."

"You are moving dangerously near to a plane of fantasy, Sergeant. May we move on to Item Five?"

"Gallows—what is the plural of gallows, Beamish? Gal-lowses? There are gallowses all over the place."

"That at least is an easy one, sir."

Beamish told him all he had learned from Mosley on the subject: the eruption of commercial interest inspired by Billy Birkin's advertisement.

"Do you mean to say, Sergeant, that this is a separate file—and that we might actually be able to close it?"

"Inspector Mosley feels uneasy about this proliferation of gallowses, sir."

"Ah, yes—Mosley. We must talk about Mosley."

"I think that Mosley is afraid that if someone is up to no good, it might be unfortunate if he came across a convenient gallows."

"Mosley *afraid*?"

"I have a strong feeling that he is in control, sir. I had the pleasure of helping him tune a piano, earlier in the day."

For an instant Grimshaw looked at Beamish as if he suspected that he was being conned. Then he appeared to shrug off the thought.

"Look at this first, then we'll talk about Mosley."

Grimshaw brought Janie Goodwin's letter out of a drawer and passed it across the table.

My Dear Jane,

What you say may be no more than I deserve. But to tell you the truth, I don't much care what I deserve. And you know me well enough, I think, to believe that I don't care.

What matters more—in fact all that matters—is that we have a common interest that transcends all other considerations. I may have got one or two things wrong about you in my time, but I would be surprised if you have not remained a realist.

It would be on the late side now to change time or

place. But if you do want to get in touch with me, B
knows how to reach me.

Yrs,

H

"So it looks as if she had an appointment," Grimshaw
said.

"Yes, sir. But was she keeping it or dodging it?"

Grimshaw gave Beamish another of his crafty looks.
Within the last few minutes, his reactions to the young
Sergeant had run through their entire gamut of possibilities. He was beginning to understand much more
clearly now why some of his narrower-minded colleagues
regarded working with Beamish as an assignment to
disaster. As far as he himself was concerned, he believed that collaboration was feasible; but only because
of the wisdom and magnanimity that came from his
experience. Grimshaw looked at his watch. Time was
pressing. They were not really achieving anything, sitting here.

"If this were your case, Beamish—" not asked as by a
man picking brains. Grimshaw's tone was brisk: the
kindly old veteran testing a novice. "—what would your
next move be?"

"Forget everything else and concentrate on the missing child."

"And the missing young woman."

"I would hope to find her in the course of the same
operation."

"Ah, yes—but what operation?"

And to Grimshaw's surprise, Beamish answered without hesitation. "I would want another talk with Mosley
before making my mind up on that."

"Ah, yes—we must not forget Mosley. I take it you've
spent a fair amount of time with him? What is his part
in all this?"

"Inactive, I would say—but not inert. He describes
himself as a catalyst."

"He said that, did he?"

"Sir."

A Grimshaw silence, in which he seemed to have retreated into a spiritual distance.

"My blood runs cold to hear you say that, Sergeant Beamish."

Beamish waited with what looked like puerile expectancy.

"Do you know why my blood runs cold when you say that, Beamish?"

"No, sir."

"Because I have heard Mosley say it before. It is a term not unfamiliar on his lips. It is when he considers that he is acting as a catalyst . . ."

The Detective-Superintendent did not finish the thought. His associations were apparently too terrible. He looked like a schoolmaster debating within himself whether to set Mosley five hundred lines: *I am not a catalyst.*

"And where precisely is our domesticated catalyst hanging out at this moment?"

"Precisely, sir, I could not say. But I do not doubt that I can find him. I think, sir, that the news of the missing child is going to shake him. I am sure that is something that he had not reckoned with."

"I'm glad you think so. You see what can come of dabbling, Beamish. This is not the first time that Mosley's catalysis has got out of hand."

"But I'm sure that his ultimate aim, sir . . ." Beamish began, not entirely abandoning his loyalty to Mosley, "I mean, he has pulled things off in his time, hasn't he?"

"Sometimes he has had luck on his side. Beamish— how long do you think it would take you to find Mosley?"

"I think I ought to allow myself a couple of hours, sir. And sir?"

"What, Beamish?"

"I would like to have a look at that sawmill first."

"It will be too dark to see anything, of course."

Grimshaw suddenly started thundering. "You think you're on to something, then have to spend half the night getting your back wheels out of a ditch. You lose your men, who are wandering about in circles."

Night operations for Grimshaw seemed to be the final realization of hell upon earth.

Beamish waited with exemplary patience for him to subside.

13

Mavis Cooke, the girl who roomed with Penny Evans, was an unknown quantity to Brakeshaft. But Penny knew her as an amateur do-gooder, a moral narcissist, a wearer of a slim-line silver crucifix in the hollow of her neck. She was also a firm believer in the purgative effect on society of mischief stirred up behind the scenes. She was a quiet, unsmiling wrecker of people's peace. And she was the last person on earth whom one would think of asking to alter her room-sharing arrangements in an obvious cause. Instead of relieving each other's nervous tension, therefore, Brakeshaft and Penny were building up frustration. Penny's other life, back in Bradburn, was not entirely uncomplicated. She would rather, in fact, have brushed off Brakeshaft altogether, than take any risk with the longer-term arrangements that she had at home.

But Brakeshaft had other ideas, and he could be persuasive: there was a strong pull that he operated when he was laying an ambush for one of his own students. He had already sampled her suppleness on a pile of old sacks in a farm shed: enough to know what she would be like in a real bed. And he had discovered an old summerhouse in the grounds of the Field Studies Centre that, like the plate-layer's hut, had afforded privacy to previous love-makers. Indeed, whoever had been the last to use it had left it more than minimally equipped. It had an old divan, even an Aladdin oil heater with a half-inch or so of fuel still swilling about in its container.

Penny Evans had done her best to keep out of Brakeshaft's reach at going-to-bed-time; she was a girl, she prided herself, who could take it or leave it, and she knew when to bow out to tactical considerations. But Brakeshaft fell in step with her as she was leaving the scrubbed-bare utility of the students' common room.

"I've found just the place."

"I've told you, Stanley—it's not on."

"Next term's internal exams, are, though, aren't they?"

"Why bring them up?"

Then suddenly she saw why; and she was a girl who could switch to a broad smile at will.

"That's how it's done, is it?"

"I'm not suggesting anything particularly wicked—just an hour or two's extra tuition beforehand. Though of course, I shall know what's going to be in the paper, because I'll have set it."

"It's all very well—I still don't trust *her*."

She jerked her head in the direction of the stairs.

"OK, then," he said. "Let's not stop out all night. You can surely cover up getting in a bit late."

So she went with him to the summerhouse—but it wasn't as it had been this morning. She rocked with him, but she gave him nothing. She had been better on the sacks than she was on the divan. And afterwards, when he was still trying to persuade her to stay, she would have none of it. He knew he would not be making love to her again—and that there would be no extra tutorials. It was about a quarter to midnight when she left him and he told himself that he would smoke one cigarette before following her out through the night. A minute and a half later he had crushed three quarters of the king-size into an old tin lid and his eyelids were drooping.

When he woke, it was cold and it took him some moments to put together where he was. He flicked his lighter to look round himself and was nauseated by a squalor of which he had not really been aware last night. He lit another cigarette and wiped the film of moisture from the glass of the window with his fingertips.

The summerhouse was set at the end of a neglected lawn that had perhaps been used formerly for croquet. Beyond that lawn he saw something for which he could think of no immediate explanation.

A car had been parked on the single-track dirt road that ran through the small park. It was an old-fashioned car, a vintage Daimler, large, black and square. Four people had got out of it, and even in his present sluggish state of mind, he could see that they too were unusual. None of them was young, but one of them in particular looked as if she belonged to a forgotten epoch. She had on a large, heavily ornamented hat and skirts so shapelessly full that it was difficult to imagine that there were limbs under them.

Brakeshaft was not an imaginative man, nor did he ever pay much attention to any detail of his environment that was not his immediate material concern. Yesterday, he knew, they had been hunting for the corpse of an old lady from the village. But he had joined in no talk about her, and had picked up nothing about her habits, reputation or description. He therefore had no reason to connect the woman out there with Miss Goodwin.

But he could not fail to pay attention to her now, for she began to conduct herself in a most peculiar way, prancing about, running up and down the shallow banks that edged the lawn, standing on one leg on a hummock as if she were improvising a clumsy ballet.

It seemed at first as if the others were taking hardly

any heed of her. Two of them were women, seemingly of the same generation as herself but dressed—and not casually, either—in clothes of the present age. Then the man in the party, formally opulent in a beige-coloured coat with leather buttons, seemed to notice for the first time how she was behaving. He said something to her which Brakeshaft could not hear, and which made her run down the hillock and swing round to give the man a view of her back and shoulders. It looked like a piece of badly hammed petulance.

The man walked back to the car, opened the rear door wider and leaned inside it with the upper half of his body. The skittish old woman then swung round again, saw where he had gone, ran after him, shouldered him out of the way and herself bent into the car, apparently doing something, Brakeshaft could not see what, to an object on the back seat.

A moment later, she took a step backwards, holding someone by the hand. It was a small child, a girl, wearing a red and white anorak, and the woman helped her out on to the side of the road. This time, Brakeshaft was in no doubt as to whom he was looking at. Detective-Superintendent Grimshaw had rapidly and widely circulated a vivid description of the vivid Brenda Shuttleworth. Brakeshaft's reaction was to step smartly back from the summerhouse window so as not to be seen. The child seemed perfectly happy with the company that she was in, but her best friend among the adults was evidently the woman in the outlandish garb, whose hand she held as they set out together towards the big house.

Brakeshaft now had to start flogging his brains. It needed no great judgement to know that this was something that had to be reported—and without delay; but he had no intention of revealing to anyone where he had spent the night. Would it make sense to claim that he had seen what he had seen from one of the windows of the house? Hardly, he thought: that would mean bringing yet someone else's bedroom into the story.

He looked at his watch: it was a quarter past six. Five minutes after she had left the group, the woman in the ancient skirts came back from the house—without the child. Did that mean that she had returned her to her quarters in the Centre?

Brakeshaft felt a surge of relief. He had been let out. There was no need for him to tell anyone anything of what he had seen.

14

From the diary of Georgina Crane for Sunday, 10 April

Elizabeth Stirrup came back this morning. It was ten minutes past five, and I doubt whether I had had more than a couple of hours' sleep myself. I thought I heard the door-knocker, but it was a very feeble effort that she was making, and God knows how many times she had had to try before she woke me.

She was almost in a faint before I could get her across the doormat, and she was quite unable to tell me anything that made continuous sense—just a few disjointed words, images, nightmare impressions: something about a gun, and God knew what they had done with the child. She would not touch alcohol. I tried to get hot soup into her, but she kept falling asleep, had hardly the strength to lift the spoon.

I practically carried her upstairs and rang Detective-Superintendent Grimshaw.

* * *

Last night Grimshaw had driven them down to the sawmill, and they had arrived just as his other two officers were about to come away in their squad car. Grimshaw made them turn back, and wasted a lot of time trying to get them to park their vehicle so that its headlamps would light up the various sectors of their search. The very thing happened that Grimshaw had spoken of less than an hour ago; they backed a rear wheel over the lip of a ditch, with a sound of metallic destruction that suggested a fractured half-shaft. That meant getting on the radio to try to drum up break-down gear—at that time of night!—and because that task devolved—abortively—on Beamish's shoulders—he was able to play very little part in the search itself. He was in fact even unable to satisfy himself that it had been carried out efficiently.

One thing stood in no doubt: they found nothing. The sawmill had not been in use for some years. Its owner had died. His heirs—with no thought of working it for themselves—had been unable to dispose of it in its derelict state, which had been made no better by a series of nasty winters and windy springs. The windows were all broken, the doors were off their hinges and a botanist's wealth of fungus had taken over timber-stocks and load-bearing joists alike. Such light as they could bring to play on the scene revealed no relic of Brenda Shuttleworth. In vain did Grimshaw's two men try to explain to him that they had been over every square yard that he insisted on going over for himself. In vain did Beamish try to make the point that it was not the sawmill at all that ought to be interesting them. Brenda Shuttleworth, he tried to remind his superior, had sim-ply crossed the sawmill site to get from where her own class was lunching to go and talk to some of her friends in another field. It was somewhere along that route that she had been sidetracked. It was therefore that route that they ought to be examining, not rotting stocks in sheds open to the elements. But it was absolutely hope-

less trying to search along that route now. That would
be to risk destroying such evidence as there might be.

Grimshaw started to become bad-tempered at being
told all this. His mind was so fully occupied with his
own ideas that little access was left for anyone else's.
Beamish was on the brink of asking him whether he
hoped to find the Assistant Chief Constable's rabbit-
skin somewhere among the lumber, but he resisted—
and determined that first thing in the morning, on his
way out to locate Mosley, he would come back here
alone and do justice to what needed justice.

At first light he was back at the sawmill. It was one of
those mornings when treacherous April had put on a
misleading allure. After yesterday's continuous rain, the
skies had cleared, and though the vegetation was sod-
den and the earth spongy in places, there was a breath
of the new season's vigour that enlivened Beamish's
lungs. He went straight to where Brenda's class had
eaten their sandwiches and found nothing. If they had
achieved nothing else from their day, these kids had
had a practical drilling in the Country Code. There was
not a paper, button or thread to record their passing.

Brenda must have passed through the grounds of the
mill to reach the next field. Beamish took that path,
looked into one or two odd corners that he had been
aching to look into last night, and again found nothing
relevant.

It was easy to see where Brenda's other friends had
eaten their *al fresco* meal. The teacher in charge of that
contingent had not been alive to the day's potential
object lessons. Beamish picked up a squashed Smarties
tube, two 7-Up tins and a single green sock. How the
hell did a child come to part company with one green
sock—and in what discomfort had she spent the rest of
her day?

He was not going to find anything vital here. He had
gleaned from the notes of the gabbled and overlapping
accounts of the other children that no one in this other

class had any memory of Brenda's arrival. Therefore it was between the sawmill and this second field that she must have been taken. Beamish found a narrow footpath, so close in under a hedge that anyone treading it would have been out of sight to the other parties for some fifty yards or so. Beamish followed that footpath. And what he found there made his private expedition worthwhile.

It was a plaited leather button of the sort worn on the superior thick overcoats worn by some army officers.

Beamish retained a very clear picture of the coat that that button had come off. Elizabeth Stirrup had been walking very close beside it, her shoulder almost tucked into its wearer's armpit. So it was Camel-hair Coat who had abducted Brenda Shuttleworth, too? For what possible reason? What wrong could a child possibly have done him? There could be only one answer: she had seen him.

And Mosley would know who Camel-hair Coat was.

Beamish came back up from the sawmill to the road with wet grasses clinging to his ankles. He must hurry to Mosley. But first, he thought, he would make a slight detour and drive slowly through Barker's Clough, to see if there were any surface indications to suggest another brief visit to the farmhouse. The more he thought about the events of yesterday morning, the more he thought that Mrs. Rawlings's home must hold the key to what was going on: his conviction that someone else had been in and about the building while he was there; and Mosley's peculiar statement that *they* must have *got her away in good time.*

Barker's Clough was lifeless in Sunday-morning somnolence, except that he could tell that the village shop, where he had bought biscuits, was open. As he passed, an elderly man came out of its door, reading the *News of the World.* Beamish drove slowly through the Clough, waiting for the severe façade of Mrs. Rawlings's farm to come into view.

It was a grim, introspective façade—and evocative. The moment he saw it, even at several hundred yards' distance, he seemed to smell again its cold, stale interior. Moreover, there was white smoke rising abundantly from one of its chimneys, and the curtains that Mosley had washed were evenly drawn back at the windows.

Beamish drove up to the house. He knew he was going to need a cover-story, and found himself unusually incapable of fabricating one: there was no telling what or whom he was going to find. He was going to have to rely on an improvisation of the moment.

The yard was in the same forsaken state that had struck him yesterday. The door of the shed which housed the Widow Rawlings's investment gallows was closed. A straggle of dejected and hungry-looking hens ran away at his approach.

He went to the door and hammered heavily. There was no response. He went and looked through one of the front windows, shielding his vision with his hands at the sides of his eyes. Within he could see a generous log fire just beginning to get up in the hearth—and at a corner of her kitchen table sat the Widow Rawlings herself, dipping a spoon into a bowl of bread and milk and reading a newspaper that lay folded in front of her. He tapped on the pane, but she did not look up. He had known that she was deaf, but had not realized that she was as deaf as this.

There was only one thing for him to do, and that was to lift the latch, a technical trespass that was likely to be vigorously resented in these parts, the one thing calculated to get him off on the wrong foot from the start. However, he had no choice. He pushed the door open just wide enough for him to see round it, giving another loud knock in attempted self-justification as he did so.

That did it. Mrs. Rawlings was on her feet at once, glowering at him. He noticed that she was glad to rest her weight on the table as she came to her feet. He also saw that her fingers were trembling.

"Oh, it's you," she said. "That young man of Mr. Mosley's. You said you'd come back, but you never did."

"I did come."

It is difficult to impress a simple fact on someone who does not hear it.

"Mr. Mosley said you'd come and put my curtains back up. He said you might iron them for me, too."

"I did come."

"It's a big job, you know, for an old woman like me. And I don't like having to stand on chairs and things."

"Mrs. Rawlings—"

"There's one thing about Mr. Mosley—if he says he's going to do a thing, he does it."

Yet the first time he had met her, she had been truculently averse to having anything done for her at all.

"Mrs. Rawlings—I *did* come."

"There's no need for you to shout."

"I did come—and you weren't here."

"I'd know what you were saying, if you didn't shout. It's the lip-reading, you know—but it only works when people speak in their ordinary voice. Oh, my God, what it is to be old!"

So he tried to form his words in a clear-cut way, but that did not seem to work either. Perhaps it made him exaggerate.

"Well—now you are here, there is a job you can do for me."

"Gladly."

"There's a sack of taters in the shed. Dick Bentham brought them yesterday, while I was out doing my bit of shopping. If you wouldn't mind carrying them into the scullery for me—"

"Gladly."

It was the shed in which he had seen the components of the gallows stacked. He looked round and saw that every single cubic foot of timber had disappeared. The shed was spaciously empty, except for the potatoes and a miscellany of spades, forks and hoes leaning under cobwebs against the walls.

Mrs. Rawlings had followed him out of the house, as if she did not trust him out of her sight. She seemed to know what he was looking for—and not finding.

"It's gone," she said. "Glad to have got it away, too—horrible thing. The man came for it yesterday afternoon, with a lorry from Bradburn."

"Oh."

"But he didn't pay me any money. I don't know how long I'm going to have to wait for my money. The lorry-driver said that was nothing to do with him."

Beamish carried the potatoes into the house and made varied attempts to direct the conversation usefully. But nothing came to anything. He could not make up his mind how much of her deafness was pretence. There were moments when she showed signs of an unexpected intelligence. Or perhaps it was only by contrast that it seemed to be intelligence. At one point, she even remembered his name from his first visit.

"If you would not mind doing one more little job for me, Mr. Beamish . . ."

But as soon as he tried to ask her a seemingly casual question about her movements yesterday—had she perhaps been out down at the shop while he had been trying to call on her?—it was impossible to make any contact with her mind at all.

The other little job took him a good deal longer than he had expected. It consisted of scrambling about in all the dirtiest and least accessible corners of the yard, under Mrs. Rawlings's nagging direction, collecting the eggs that her hens seemed to lay wherever they fancied. He undertook it because he hoped that further willingness might unloose willingness on her part. But it didn't. She was clearly on the point of remembering something else that she wanted done, when he managed to back away from her towards his car.

Of course, he could ask in the shop. He had made reasonable progress in there, the first time he had come to the Clough. He could find out at what time yesterday, if at all, Mrs. Rawlings had come in for her groceries.

He had to wait a long time for attention. The only customer in front of him was a small child buying sweets, but the woman behind the counter was giving as much attention to the choice between sherbet balls and spearmint chews as she would have done to the visit of a Health Inspector.

When Beamish's turn came, it was obvious that she recognized him at once, for she reached up to a shelf behind her and handed him a sealed letter.

It was from Mosley, and consisted mainly of a list of domestic favours that he begged Beamish to do today on his behalf.

Because by the time you read this, I shall be well on my way to East Africa.

15

"She's just about as sound constitutionally as any young woman I've ever examined."

That was Dr. Moulton's verdict on Elizabeth Stirrup.

"Heart and lungs as sound as I'd prescribe for one of her age. And not a bruise or scratch on her. But obviously she's been in some sort of war . . ."

He looked quizzically at Georgina Crane. Elizabeth Stirrup hardly seemed to know that she was being examined.

"You may have heard of her in the news. She's one of the two who disappeared. She came back in this state."

"Let her sleep it out. See what she's like when she wakes. I'll pass by this way again this evening. In the meantime, if you're worried, give me a ring."

Beamish did not believe that Mosley had left the country. Nor would he have guaranteed at this moment that his earlier admiration for the Inspector was going to survive this latest bout of imbecility. Moreover, he believed that there were plenty of people in this neighbourhood who knew very well that Mosley had not gone to Kenya, and who could, if they saw fit, reveal his whereabouts at the drop of a hat. But no hat was going to be dropped. Mosley would have seen to that. His ridiculous headgear was wedged firmly down to the tips of his obstinate ears. There was a persistent image at the back of Beamish's brain: it was of the stumpy little Mosley, homburg, raincoat and all, hiding behind every bank of heather, every slither of boulders and every screen of gorse, watching his, Beamish's, every movement. And, here and there, Mosley would have planted clues, indications as to where he wanted him to go toiling off to next.

There was only one thing to do, and that was to pursue the list of chores that Mosley had bequeathed him. Because it was somewhere on the flanks of that pilgrimage that Mosley would be lurking. But Beamish knew he would have to continue to work on the woman who ran the shop. She was clearly an ally of Mosley's and firmly under his thumb—but there might be some way of tricking her into giving something away. The first time Beamish had met her, he had managed to get information out of her by patient subterfuge. He was just about to ask her a vital question now when someone else came into the shop. Like a well-trained commercial traveller, Beamish stood back to give priority to a local customer. It was a decrepit veteran pauper in bedroom slippers who wanted to buy a single rasher of smoked back bacon. This the woman declined to sell him, informing him that it was against the law to sell on the Sabbath a foodstuff that required preparation for the table. At the same time she made elaborate facial signs to try to let him know that the law was on the premises. And good God! Beamish thought—does she think I have nothing better to do than come between a man and his breakfast?

"Why don't you promise her in front of a witness," he suggested, "that you are going to eat it raw."

"Oh, aye—allus do," the man said. He got his rasher, for which the shopkeeper had to broach a prepacked plastic bag. Beamish was left alone in the shop.

"Was there something else, then, Mr. Beamish?"

Beamish was certain that he had never told her his name. She could have had it only from Mosley. And she had remembered it.

"Yes—about Mr. Mosley—he didn't leave me any verbal message?"

"No—he just dropped in last night—after he'd brought Mrs. Rawlings back. And he's gone now to spend a few days with his sister, you know—hasn't seen her for seventeen years. He'd just had a message from the airport about his reservation."

"Just a moment—did you say he had brought Mrs. Rawlings back from somewhere?"

"Yes. She'd spent the day with her grandniece, over at Lower Calesthorpe."

"Had he taken her there too, yesterday morning?"

"Oh, I couldn't say about that. But I do know that he brought her home again."

"I see. What time was this?"

"Oh, it would be between six and seven in the evening."

"And when was his flight? Did he mention that?"

"Oh, no—and I didn't want to seem inquisitive. It was none of my business."

"He didn't say which airport?"

"No, he never mentioned anything like that."

No—he wouldn't, would he, the wily old basket.

"It's funny, you know," she volunteered. "There were a lot of strange faces in the Clough yesterday."

"Oh, ah?"

"There was this big old black car—I'd seen that in the morning, too. Then it was back again only a second or two after Mr. Mosley had left."

"What kind of big old black car?"

"Oh, very ancient—but spick and span—like as if it had escaped from some transport museum. I suppose there was a rally somewhere. The people in it looked like gentry of the old sort, too. Two women, a man and a little girl."

"And you say they followed hard on Inspector Mosley's heels?"

"Oh, yes—there was hardly a moment between them."

"So you'd say that Mr. Mosley must have seen them?"

"I don't see how he could have missed them. They must have been getting out of their car as he was getting into his."

Sunday morning, I'm taking two old ladies to chapel at Higher Stonely.

So Mosley had said—and their names and directions for finding their house were duly to be found in his letter to Beamish.

It was a fair drive to Higher Stonely, which lay at the north-western extremity of Mosley's kingdom. The two old ladies—Miss Lois and Miss Laetitia Ledman—were as Beamish expected two compulsive chapel-goers to be; but there were things about their home that were out of character. As to appearances Laetitia was tall, gaunt and undernourished. Lois was apparently the one who accounted for most of the household's rations, being short, round, well-fleshed and beaming. Both spoke in thin, apologetic voices, rich in local vowels but extremely precise in their enunciation. Their gratitude at being taken to the next village for morning worship was embarrassingly repetitious. Their clothes belonged to the period between the wars—though not of the same vintage as Janie Goodwin's: they had at least emerged from the 1920s—if only just. They must have found some friendly neighbourhood hairdresser who had reached the prime of her skills long before the Silver Jubilee of King George and Queen Mary. Miss Laetitia had clumps at the side of her head in the fashion that used to be known as ear-phones, while Miss Lois's coiffure seemed to date from the original introduction of the permanent wave, which clung tightly and whitely to the contours of her head.

The walls of their house were appropriately adorned with comforting texts, and an evangelistic hymnbook stood open on the rack of a piano that had presumably so far escaped Mosley's specialized attentions. But these things apart, there were possessions in their sitting-room that Beamish looked at twice.

For example, the sisters owned a small and relatively inexpensive but none the less contemporary personal computer, and the manual on the table beside it suggested that one or both of them took an active interest in data-management systems. Most of their furniture was old, and some of it antique but without consistency of taste or co-ordination of impact. And in one corner, between a bamboo-matting table and a revolving book-stand in fumed oak, stood a three-tier suspension filing-cabinet in green metal. The pink newsprint of the *Financial Times* was prominent among the contents of a wicker magazine-rack.

Time was advancing, and Beamish took them straight to their chapel without much time for constructive talk. He did not go into the service with them, truthfully pleading that he had urgent telephone calls to make.

These started at the main information desk of Manchester Ringway, and led him eventually to Heathrow, where he learned from a passenger manifest that a man called Mosley had taken off for Nairobi with Air Kenya at seven this morning.

On the way home with his two passengers, Beamish

was too full of difficult thoughts for conversation in depth. There were things that he needed to work out, but instead of coming up with solutions, his brain kept circling round them. He still did not want to believe that Mosley had gone, and his mind did not want to come to grips with the likely consequences if the old man had in fact deserted. He told himself that it was by no means beyond Mosley's resources to have fixed the Air Kenya desk to give false information. But if the bird had indeed flown—and if he could be implicated as an accessory in the disappearance of a woman and a girl—then the prospects would not bear contemplation: Beamish could not forget that there had been a time when he had had quite an affection for Mosley.

An April shower hit the windscreen, then the cloud that had produced it was gone. His two passengers burbled on. There was no doubt that this morning had been a true spiritual experience for them, and they could not keep their elation to themselves. Beamish was glad he had taken them: the halo-consciousness of the do-gooder who sees something for his pains. He changed into third gear to negotiate the bends of a falling valley whose greenery was beginning to attest the freshness of spring. And he managed to keep up a polite end in the conversation without at first paying very deep attention to it. The thought also occurred to him that under their rather pathetic effervescence, the two sisters might possibly be building up to telling him something.

"It's not every day of the week that something like this happens to us," Miss Lois giggled.

"I say good old Inspector Mosley!" Miss Laetitia chortled.

"I can still hardly believe it has happened."

"That sum Inspector Mosley did about the compound interest was the finishing touch."

"Quite the finishing touch."

"We must put it in the computer and see if he got it right."

"Oh, you can be sure he got it right. Inspector Mosley doesn't make mistakes about things like that."

"Or about anything else if you ask me."

"Don't you think Inspector Mosley is a wonderful man, Mr. Beamish?"

"Oh, quite remarkable," Beamish said, aware that his tone might be lacking in the unqualified enthusiasm that the women clearly expected of him. It was also now obvious to him that they were no longer talking about the uplift of the service that they had just attended.

"But then, of course, you'll have been in on this all along the line, won't you, Mr. Beamish?"

"Oh, yes—we work together a good deal of the time," Beamish said.

"Now, of course, we've got to put our heads together and decide what to do with it all."

"If you put it into unit trusts, there's no telling how much of it goes into breweries and cigarette firms."

"I thought there was going to be a fight, though, at one time."

"Those two men—I felt sure they were going to come to blows."

"Miss Goodwin was a tower of strength from start to finish."

"I shall never forget the look on Ernie Walton's face. I don't think he's ever had his hands on so much money at one time in his life."

"And Mr. Mosley said that even compound interest didn't compensate for all these years of inflation."

"Still—we mustn't grumble."

"Ernie Walton certainly wasn't grumbling."

And the sisters laughed together as if they were auditioning for a scene on a blasted heath.

"Look," Beamish said. "You must tell me what exactly did happen yesterday. I've not seen Mosley since, and I'm not up to date."

"Oh—in that case—I don't know whether we ought—"

"I don't know whether Mr. Mosley would want us to—"

"He did say he wouldn't care for everybody to know how he sometimes sets about things."

" 'Right hand, left hand,' he said."

"Perhaps you'd better wait until you see Mr. Mosley again, Mr. Beamish."

"On the other hand," Beamish said, his brain driven as by pistons, "our friend Mosley has gone away, you know."

"Oh, yes—he told us all about that."

"All the way to Africa."

"And he's left me to tie up all the loose ends for him. He asked me to clear everything up when I saw you this morning."

They seemed to need a few tens of seconds to chew all this over. He was conscious of rhythmical breathing on the seat behind him. The Misses Ledman were hemmed in by a formidable palisade of suspicion. He could not be certain how intelligent they were—but their elemental shrewdness was frightening. They had an all-embracing instinct for self-protection.

"Well—I don't know what we are going to be able to tell you," Lois said. "I don't think we did know what was happening to us half the time."

"I certainly didn't," Laetitia said.

"But of course we'll tell you all we do know. You must come in for a glass of ginger wine when we get home."

They were aggressive teetotallers, but the ginger wine was something more than a concession, it was—they both said it—a proof to the world that they were not bigoted. They produced the bottle with proud panache and poured Beamish a tot as if they were handing him something that they knew he was craving for. During the course of the next hour, he learned a good deal. But the more he learned, the more conscious he was of essential gaps in his knowledge.

The first thing that they insisted on his knowing was that their father had been a bank clerk, and they produced this ancestral achievement as if he had sat on half the boards in Threadneedle Street. This was the financial basis on which their own lifelong business acumen rested. They were not well off: this fact had been established early on in a kind of self-defence, as if it would make it less likely that Beamish would try to beg or steal from them. But they had a certain small sum between them. They were coy at first about how much it was—but like all the things they were coy about, it was something that they were eager to announce after the appropriate dramatic build-up.

Together they had two thousand pounds. And they had invested it all over the market, in small sums that gave them a compulsive interest in the daily movements of shares: fifty pounds in a department store here, one hundred and fifty in a chain chemist there, nominal holdings in municipalities in all quarters of the realm. They were showered with balance sheets, received more invitations to AGMs than many a fiscal giant.

"And, of course, it does make sure the postman calls."

"And we can check the figures so much faster, now we have this thing."

A gesture in the direction of their computer.

"Though of course we don't make use of all the things it can do."

"We do at least know how to make it add up."

But as well as their portfolios, they had one notional asset. There was a history of bad debt—something that they admitted they had long since given up any hope of retrieving, but that they had always included in their annual accounts for accuracy's sake. Wilson Goodwin Senior had owed their father fifty pounds. It was characteristic of Goodwin that having had a request for a renewal of overdraft turned down in the inner office, he had at least managed to raise a puff of wind from a mere ledger clerk. But then, that was one of the reasons why Wilson Goodwin had survived at all. There was something about him that made all sorts of unexpected people get satisfaction from helping him out of temporary holes.

The debt had not been repaid until yesterday, and—at this stage the narrative of the Misses Ledman began to become vague—this was something that Mosley had initiated. A few weeks ago, Mosley had been round at the Ledmans' house asking questions and, while promising nothing, had dropped a few optimistic hints.

Janie Goodwin came into the picture somewhere, though Beamish was unable to find out—because the Ledmans did not know—whether it was as a prime mover. There were also two men involved in the story somewhere. They had both been at the meeting that Mosley had taken the sisters to attend yesterday. One of them they knew—because that was how he was addressed—was Janie Goodwin's brother, a reprobate of whom they had heard, but whom they had never met.

"The strange thing is, you'd have thought he was such a nice man."

"A gentleman, you'd have said."

But they were able to give Beamish only the most disappointing account of the other man, amounting only to a physical description, which was remarkable only for the outdoor coat he was wearing.

"Where did all this take place?"

"Oh, I wouldn't like to try to tell you that."

"Do you know, we've lived in these parts all our lives, and there are some places we've still never seen?"

"It was so wild."

"Like *Wuthering Heights*."

"That woman, screaming upstairs."

"That wasn't *Wuthering Heights*, Lois—that was *Jane Eyre*."

"What woman, screaming up what stairs?" Beamish asked them.

"She was a young woman. I think they'd brought her with them. I think they'd locked her up somewhere."

"There was a little girl, too. Miss Goodwin was very nice to her."

"So was Inspector Mosley."

"Just a minute," Beamish said.

The women had in their minds a montage of crisply felt but inexplicable mysteries, of which they were only now beginning to relish the full flavour. They had clearly had to do with Janie Goodwin, Elizabeth Stirrup, Brenda Shuttleworth, Wilson Goodwin Junior, the man in the camel-hair coat—and Mosley.

"Where did all this happen?"

Beamish was striving not to allow impatience to creep into his tone: it would be all too easy to scare them off.

"We've been beating our brains against that. Lois is sure it was east of here."

"And Laetitia is certain the sun was mostly behind us."

"We went round so many corkscrews."

"I'm sure the driver was doubling back on himself on purpose."

"It was miles from anywhere."

"It wasn't big enough to call a village. Perhaps it hasn't even got a name."

"There can't have been more than half a dozen houses."

It had to be Barker's Clough.

"Then when the man came about the gallows—"

"He looked just like the public hangman."

"Laetitia, that's very loose talk. You know you've never seen the public hangman."

"No, but you know what I mean. This man drove up in a hurry, Mr. Beamish. And he asked where the gallows was."

"And we weren't the only ones who thought he'd come to do something dreadful."

"Wilson Goodwin certainly thought he had."

"And Inspector Mosley was looking on with a sort of twisted, knowing smile."

"Like a sort of cherubic Beelzebub," Lois Ledman said.

"Oh, come now, Lois—that's going a bit far."

There was more like this—a good deal more like it. A good deal of it fitted in with what Beamish already knew, but it did very little to extend that knowledge—or to help him to interpret it.

Beamish went back to Mosley's letter to remind himself of the remainder of the day. It was clearly no mere flight of chance that his next call had to be on Ernie Walton who, according to the Ledman sisters, had figured very highly in the distribution of funds over which Mosley had presided yesterday.

Cabbages in plastic bucket in shed was the instruction that Mosley had included in his notes on Neighbouring.

Beamish found those plants, done up in newspaper and string in the yellow receptacle described. He did not claim horticultural expertise. Such lore as he had on the subject had come from other men's complaints against their own folly in attempting to till the soil at all in such an area. But even Beamish could see that these waifs and foundlings from other men's thinnings-out were not worth the trouble of preparing a bed for them. There was about them a limp weariness, a perforated yellow wilt that did not prognosticate survival. One did not need the cross-references of a *Reader's Digest* vademecum to recognize an early inclination to club root, the fatal evidence of early frost damage and an obvious propensity to grey mould, leaf spot and soft rot.

"Did Mosley get these for you?"

"Aye."

It would be too much to say that Ernie Walton showed pride in his pailful of green weaklings. But he did not show dissatisfaction with them, which was curious. Ernie Walton was not a man who ever revealed pride—or, indeed, anything else so debilitating as a human emotion—but his normal conversation was a comprehensive, far-ranging and everlasting statement of dissatisfaction with everything. His only reaction to any circumstance was to distrust it. And certainly he distrusted Beamish. He asked him more than once, and in a variety of ways, whether he was sure that he was the man that Mosley had sent. Ernie Walton was a little man, in his early seventies, like so many of the principals in this action, and he wore clothes whose chances of seeing the year out were about on the par of those of his cabbage plants.

Beamish decided that the only thing to do was to get on with the job as if it were serving some useful purpose. A swashbuckling spade and a touch of bravado with the dibber would all help to lessen the time that the job would take. Ernie Walton fetched a backless kitchen chair from his shed and sat on it at the end of his patch, watching every one of Beamish's amateurish movements and registering grounds for complaint the next time he saw Mosley.

It could be said of this particular acreage of allotments that Ernie's cabbages, once deployed, would not look out of place. The grey, stony soil, liberally laced also with riddled cinders, was the sort of environment that these tender plantlings had grown up in. By the time that Beamish had come to the end of his third and final row, a number of other weekend gardeners had also left their last ostensible occupation and were dotted about their earthy paths silently watching. Beamish put in the last sorry herb, pressed the soil firmly against its feeble stem with his heel, and stood back to survey Ernie Walton's investment in the seasonal future. The leaves of some thirty plants were lying flat on the ground, at the end of stalks that looked like discarded vermicelli.

"Poor little buggers!" he heard some one say.

He scraped soil off the spade, wound up Ernie's sack-tie line and carried the bits and pieces back into Ernie's shed.

"Well, there you are, Ernie. Don't blame me if some of them don't make it. Get in touch with Mosley."

Ernie looked at him with an ugly eye, as if the very

superfluity of speech was some guide to what its content might have been.

"Did Mr. Mosley not say owt about any money?"

"Not to me, he didn't. But I gather you did rather well out of yesterday's readjustments. Quite a few outstanding debts were settled, I'm told."

"Oh, you were told, were you?"

Once Ernie Walton had taken to doubting, it was difficult to utter any single syllable without further nourishing that doubt.

"You saw the Inspector last night, I take it, after he'd finished with us?"

"Well, no—he left me a letter."

Ernie's suspicion deepened. Nothing was quite as untrustworthy as the written word.

"Forty pounds," he said, with a sinister insinuation. "You're sure Mr. Mosley didn't say owt about forty pounds?"

"Do you think I'd hide it from you if he had? Look—you don't doubt me, do you? Mosley told you it would be me who'd come today, didn't he?"

"He said it would be a bright young fellow, very much on the ball."

"There are one or two things I'd like to ask you about yesterday."

"Oh, aye? Well, you'd better ask Mosley, hadn't you?"

By now Ernie had firmly decided that Beamish must be entirely on the wrong side of the fence.

"This is altogether a complicated business," Beamish said.

"Aye—well, some of that forty pounds went to pay off the bloke who came for the gallows, Emma Rawlings being out, and not having left anything in the tea-caddy. And Mosley needed the rest to settle out-of-pocket expenses—so he said. He'd let me have the rest later. That's all I can tell you. And I don't know how it comes about that you don't know these things for yourself, if you're who you say you are."

And that was the tenor of the remainder of Beamish's talk with Ernie Walton. He decided that the time had come, much as he would have liked to put it off, to make another report to Detective-Superintendent Grimshaw.

16

Georgina Crane looked at Elizabeth Stirrup's face as it lay valleyed in the pillows, in final surrender to exhaustion. How was it possible that such a quick-brained and above all else industrious child should have turned into this useless creature? The most sobering thought was that perhaps she had positively striven to turn herself into the end-product that she thought her teachers wanted her to be.

Georgina went to her window and looked out over the village. It was the same April morning on which Sergeant Beamish had started out in the vanished wake of Mosley: a freshness in the air and a fair sky for the first time for days, with only shower-clouds moving fast over the horizon. She had a view of Hempshaw End that would perhaps not have appealed to many landscape painters, but she saw a positive beauty in the random cast of roofs and chimneys. And she saw that from one of those chimneys, smoke was rising: from Janie Goodwin's.

She put on her outdoor coat, let herself silently out of the house, and made for Janie Goodwin's. When she was almost there, she had a change of mind, turned face-about and climbed the hill towards Noll Cromwell's.

As if by some masochistic intuition, Grimshaw came awake a full minute before his bedside phone rang: long enough for him to reassemble in his mind the expectation that today was going to be worse than yesterday. There were times when Grimshaw wished he had embraced some other career: raking up elephant dung in some under-capitalized travelling circus, for example.

And who would be phoning him at this pre-dawn stand-to hour? The Assistant Chief Constable, perhaps, proffering some overnight hunch about where he might lay his hands on that rabbit-skin?

It was the Warden of the Field Studies Centre, informing him of the unharmed return of Brenda Shuttleworth. His better nature told him that this was a moment for silent thanksgiving. But his mind, more active on a less noble stratum, was filled with the illogical feeling that the news could signify only that something else, somewhere else, must have gone wrong. It could not be straightforward good news. Somebody, somewhere, must have buggered something up. It had, of course, to be Mosley; but there was yet another cloud-shadow on Grimshaw's horizon nowadays; it might equally easily have been Beamish. Grimshaw drove through the Sunday-morning streets of one of Bradburn's most desirable dormitory suburbs, feeling nothing but venom towards the visible and outward signs of bourgeois complacency all round him.

Why this unreason? Why not unmitigated relief that the child was still alive? The Warden had insisted that she was in the pink of condition. *A little child shall lead us.* Maybe a little child was going to clear up the whole issue for him; rendering him, of course, superfluous.

Brenda was sleeping the sleep of the innocent when

Grimshaw arrived at Hempshaw End. And there had to
be a strong-willed Matron in attendance to whom it
seemed inhuman that anyone should think of disturbing
the child. Grimshaw hovered at the bedside wishing to
God that somebody would make an accidental noise.
But Brenda slept loglike, an unaesthetic bubble quiver-
ing in the corner of her mouth.

As far as a fairly superficial examination could ascer-
tain, she was quite unhurt; Grimshaw the professional
insisted that she was to be taken off to Casualty for
unmentionable investigation as soon as he had finished
with her: that was if he was ever going to be allowed to
start. She had come back to the Centre, those about
her informed him, in very high spirits indeed, not so
much, they had to admit, through relief at being back
among her own kind, but in elation at the things that
had happened to her in her absence. She had said
something about an old woman and a ride in a pre-
deluge but *super* car. Both woman and car had conve-
niently disappeared by the time Brenda's return was
known to the staff of the Centre.

It was getting on for mid-morning when she woke,
and her first reaction was to cry, presumably in expia-
tion of her supposed naughtiness. Advisers at all levels
quickly put her right on that score and Grimshaw was
eventually able to question her as she sat up in bed
dipping her spoon into a boiled egg.

Common ground was that she had gone off from the
field by the sawmill to try to find some friends from the
Second Year in the next sector. Under cover of a hedge
down by the derelict woodyard, she had run into a
person who could only, from her description, have been
Janie Goodwin, with whom she had quickly made friends.
Tut-tut that any child from a school frequently visited
by crime-prevention officers should go off alone with
an adult stranger. But children did go off with adult
strangers, however often one lectured them, Brenda
Shuttleworth was obviously just such a child. And

there was no doubt that the adult stranger in this case had made herself very plausible indeed. Successful abductors generally are.

Little bits of the jigsaw came together. Brenda Shuttleworth had lingered for a long time in an entertaining conversation with Janie Goodwin—for such a long time that they both failed to realize that the school party had moved on. Janie therefore said that if Brenda came with her, she would ring up the Centre to let them know that she was in good hands, and that she would organize transport to take her back to her friends. She herself did not want to get caught by the search-party—it would spoil a game that she and some of her grown-up friends were playing. She had so far evaded capture by moving forward on the extreme edge of the search-line, so far from the others that they could not recognize even the weirdness of her costume. Twice in fact, much to her amusement—and Brenda laughed again as she retold it to Grimshaw—a policeman had spotted her from a distance and beckoned her to move in closer to the cordon.

Before they moved off from the shelter of the hedge, Janie Goodwin had taken from her pocket an old-fashioned-looking overcoat button, which she had thrown down on the path behind them. It was all part of the game, she told the child, which was a sort of grown-up hide-and-seek. And Brenda knew that grown-ups did sometimes play games. Her aunties and uncles played Murder and Sardines all over the house at Christmas. Everybody was looking for the man in the coat that the button had come off, and when they found this button here, they would all think—quite wrongly—that he had come this way.

Brenda was able to tell Grimshaw very little else. They had walked up to a crossroads where a car was waiting for them, and it had driven them up to an old and rather dirty farmhouse where there were a lot of adults, most of them according to Brenda very *old*, who were having some sort of meeting in a downstairs room. These were the only unhappy two hours in Brenda's day's experience, because Janie Goodwin unaccountably switched off her friendliness for the time being and shut her in an upstairs room which she shared with a woman—Brenda was not perceptive enough to call her young—who proved to be uneasy company. *Ferrety* was the word that Brenda used to describe her. But she was by no means as felicitous in her descriptions of the other people whom she saw about that house. They seemed to have been an extremely nondescript crew. The only one who had made a vivid impression on her was a short, stocky man in a black hat and a raincoat that did not seem to have any buttons. But she said that he was not there long. She just saw him come and go late in the afternoon, and did not think that he was in the house longer than about a quarter of an hour. Grimshaw managed to suppress his emotions of every kind.

And that was all that coaxing, cajoling and suggestion could get from Brenda Shuttleworth. He came away from the Centre unconvinced that he had gained anything at all by talking to the child.

He also found Elizabeth Stirrup sitting up in bed— and likewise applying herself to a boiled egg. And there came into Grimshaw's mind a picture of himself lying propped up against Sunday-morning pillows with a spoiled man's breakfast on a tray in front of him.

Elizabeth Stirrup smiled at him. It was a thin smile, one in which only a deprived optimist would have seen any hint of come-hither. But from their previous, admittedly brief meetings, it was one smile more than Grimshaw had hitherto judged her capable of. Georgina Crane was lingering between him and the bedroom door, and he could see that she would have needed very little encouragement to stay through the coming interview. He reluctantly gave her a very hostile look, whose meaning she grasped at once.

"Shall I make coffee, Superintendent?"

"Perhaps later on, please, Miss Crane."

Miss Crane withdrew. Miss Stirrup looked irretrievably washed-out—in marked contrast to Brenda Shuttleworth's resilient freshness.

"I'm sorry to come disturbing your much-needed rest like this, Miss Stirrup. But if you wouldn't mind filling in a few missing details for me—"

"Oh, no. Please ask anything you like. I'm afraid I've been a bit silly—but apart from that, I fear I've nothing exciting to tell you."

"Well, let's start at the beginning, shall we? Tell me how you came to leave this place in the first instance."

"Well—I left it. It's as simple as that, really. I'd made up my mind I had to get away from Hempshaw End. I didn't feel I could stand the place half an hour longer. It had all started with the shock of last Friday dinner time, and then there was the search-party— and I must say I hated to see the children being dragged into that. I was stupid, I suppose, but I felt that I absolutely had to get away."

She looked at him wide-eyed—the eyes of a very ingenuous young woman, of a young woman whose life had been unbelievably sheltered. How could any girl have managed that in this part of this century?

"So I decided to ring the garage, to see if they had a car that would take me to Bradburn Station, but I couldn't get any reply."

"They were all out with me, searching the hills."

"That's what I discovered. But I thought at first it just might mean that their office was not manned, so I decided to walk down there and see if I could find anyone. And that's where I ran into a motorist who was trying in vain to get attention on the forecourt. I told him what my problem was, and he said he had to make a detour, to call on some friends in the hills, but that he would take me to Bradburn if I didn't mind the delay."

"Can you describe this man?"

Camel-hair Coat.

"You took a dangerous chance, accepting that kind of lift, Miss Stirrup."

"Oh, I know that. If I didn't know it for myself, Georgina has left me in no doubt. But I can't describe to you how desperate I was to get away. Besides—he seemed a very civilized type of man—and turned out to be one."

"And where did he take you to? Where was this place in the hills?"

"I couldn't begin to tell you. There's such a sameness. To my eyes this is all such a wilderness. One hill's so much like another, there are no signposts, and the sky was so cloudy that I couldn't see where the sun was."

"Well—try to describe the place itself—the house you were taken to."

"A farmhouse, I suppose—but it didn't seem much of a farm. There was some sort of family party going on—not at all hilarious, you understand—more like a family conference than a party. And it went on a lot longer than was expected. Which was why I wasn't brought back until during the night."

She looked at him hopefully—her hope being that he was going to believe her. She was a very poor liar indeed—inexperienced, he guessed, in the most elementary deceit.

"Am I supposed to believe all that you've told me, Miss Stirrup?"

"I shall be most offended if you don't."

A truly schoolmistressly yap.

"There was a small child at this party, who was not supposed to be there, Miss Stirrup."

"I know. And that worried me at first. But she could not have been better looked after, I assure you. She was only there because she had become parted from her school group, and Miss Goodwin had taken her in tow. And she was extremely happy most of the time."

"Only *most* of it?"

"Both she and I were excluded from the family conference. We were locked away from the others while that was on. I must confess I was worried myself at that stage."

"And at encountering Miss Goodwin, I would have thought."

"Not really. Apart from her peculiar dress-sense, she is a most natural person."

"Didn't you ask her what she was doing there? What had happened in her cottage last Friday?"

"At no stage was I alone with her."

"What was the family conference about? You were able to form any impressions?"

"None at all."

"You overheard nothing?"

"Nothing at all."

"You picked up no hints?"

"None, Superintendent."

"How very convenient."

"I do not like your tone, Superintendent."

"And I do not care to be obstructed. I shall be back here during the course of today. I hope it will not be necessary to take you elsewhere for questioning, Miss Stirrup."

Elizabeth Stirrup, Grimshaw felt, was simply at the moment trying to play an old-timer's game that she would never be able to keep up. She would be the easiest one to trap—his easiest way into the core of the case. But there was no point in sitting storming at her in her present obdurate mood—likely to dissolve into a sickness plea at any moment. He had to build up his background knowledge as fully as he could from anyone who could give him any. Then would be the time, fully primed, to put the pressure on Miss Elizabeth Stirrup.

He had taken the hint from her that Janie Goodwin might also now be back home. He looked for and saw smoke from Janie's chimney as soon as he rounded the corner that brought it in view. Janie's living-room had been tidied up, and she was sitting in front of a homely fire with Noll Cromwell. Cromwell was in the same Sunday best as he had worn to make his nocturnal call on Georgina Crane. The pair were drinking Bloody Marys. Grimshaw declined a glass.

"It's looking a little different from when I last saw it," he said, taking in the room with a sweep of his eyes. He was pretty sure now that somehow, for some reason, she and Cromwell were entirely responsible for everything that had happened. But he did not want to accuse them yet of wasting police time. It would be better to trip them into some self-incriminatory remark that would lead him into it.

"You'll have to let us know for the record your precise evaluation of the damage."

"No damage at all," Janie said.

She had a cultured voice, but it had none of the aggression of the Home Counties giantess. There was, he noticed more and more in the next few minutes, a gentleness about all her manners and attitudes. It contrasted very sharply with all he had led himself to expect of her.

"No damage at all? Why—the place was a perfect shambles."

"A few pieces of furniture knocked over, sir."

Even the "sir" had a subtlety of its own. It was far from insolent—but it was a reminder that she hailed from a different world: where "sirs" were as commonplace as they were *de rigueur*.

"A settee lying on its back. The legs of a chair mixed up with those of another. It does create an impression of chaos, I agree."

"I saw a very large Wedgwood pot in fragments."

"Oh—that's been broken for years. Hasn't it, Noll?"

Cromwell nodded with exasperating sobriety. "Oh, yes. It fell off its bracket in the earthquake, Superintendent."

"Earthquake? What earthquake?"

"It was a slight tremor we had in the 1950s. It didn't

make headlines. I don't think you were here in those days."

Grimshaw examined the pair of them silently for a quarter of a minute.

"Are you preparing the ground for the pretence that nothing untoward has been happening in the Hemp Valley?"

Janie Goodwin looked at him with a hint that there might be a system of steel springs somewhere beneath the gentility. "Do you think it brings me pleasure when this sort of thing happens, Superintendent? Such care was taken not to break anything that I can only look on it as some sort of prank."

Including rabbit's blood and sheep's wool?

"And what about the fish in the window?" Grimshaw asked.

Mosley had sent a cryptic message via Beamish about the fish in the window. Grimshaw thought he saw the point now. The fish had been put there because it had been absolutely essential to get the hue and cry on the heels of the missing Janie Goodwin without any delay.

"You are looking at me in a peculiar way," Janie said.

"I'd like to see you draw a fish, Miss Goodwin."

"Mrs. Cromwell."

He knew, of course, that he was a fool. He had spoiled what chances, if any, the ploy might have had. If he were to look round now for pencil and paper, she'd take good care that her sketch wouldn't match the one that had been in the window.

"They tried to get me into that fish scheme a couple of years ago, but I wouldn't play. It's only an excuse for busybodies to get into your home. I'm sorry if you feel we're wasting your time, Superintendent. But I've not laid any complaint and I shan't be laying any."

"Unfortunately, processes aren't stopped as easily as that, Mrs. Cromwell. There's the matter of abducting a child."

"Abducting her? She stopped to talk to me: is that an

offence? Then we found that her friends had made off without her, so I made sure she got back to them."

"So how would you react to a charge of illegal detention? You kept her locked in a room."

"Only for her own safety, Superintendent."

"For her safety? What was going on to need locked-door protection?"

"Nothing. Nothing much happened—as it turned out."

"But you are admitting that you were engaged in something you wouldn't care for us to know about?"

"Not at all. What was going on was perfectly legal—so legal that you people could have cleared it up forty years ago."

"Only it's difficult to clear things up when you haven't even heard of them," Cromwell said—and looked as if he felt he had scored a point. "Come to that, you don't even know about it *yet*."

"I'm sorry if we seem to be making life difficult for you, Superintendent," Janie said. "I know how very much you would like to solve a great crime. Well, unfortunately, we can't provide you with one. Not even a little one. There hasn't been a crime, Mr. Grimshaw."

For the next twenty minutes or so there was parry and thrust of the same sort of specious debate, until it became repetitive—and very obviously fruitless. He could only say what he had said to Elizabeth Stirrup: He would be back.

"You're not going to the big show, then, Superintendent?" Cromwell asked him, as he was preparing to leave.

"Big show?"

"They're hanging Crippen at Sarah Bramwell's at eleven. There's likely to be quite a crowd: everybody worth knowing. What is it they call it—the police presence? I'm sure there'd be a strong case for a police presence."

17

Brenda Shuttleworth stood—with both feet—on the threshold of puberty; and observers of all kinds attest that puberty is happening at a younger age these days than in the earlier years of this century. But whether they are standing before, upon or beyond that threshold, young people travelling on chartered coaches often disappoint their adult escorts when it comes to the appreciation of scenery.

Brenda Shuttleworth—and the rest of her class—were no exception. As their coach pulled out of Hempshaw End, their eyes were not lifted unto the hills. But if they did chance to catch sight of them, the help they received was at least basically similar to the reactions of the psalmist: they sang. They sang in unison but out of tune, any element of close harmony quite involuntary. Their rhythm was insistent, but they omitted any attempt at the syncopation that had first attracted them to the original.

Except Brenda Shuttleworth. Brenda did not sing. She talked. She sat telling her friend Mavis many things which Detective-Superintendent Grimshaw would have loved to have coaxed out of her.

"There was a great love in her life," Brenda said, with a natural mixture of solemnity and matter-of-factness that would have impressed Mavis with her sincerity, if Mavis had been the sort of child who questioned such things.

"He was a cousin, or something. A cousin, I think. And you know how it is with cousins. You don't even notice them half the time, and when Miss Goodwin was a girl, and used to live at the Field Studies Centre, she and this cousin used to pass each other in the grounds and not even see each other. But then she went abroad."

They had just crossed a bridge over one of the upper reaches of the Old Railway. A sheep ran in front of their bus for some yards, bringing their speed down to a walking pace.

"She was with another lady, an old lady, who was absolutely rolling in money. And they went round looking at churches and ruins and art galleries and that. And they stayed at fabulous hotels, and then this cousin of hers turned up, and this time they did notice each other."

The sheep finally side-stepped up a bank and disappeared through a gap in a dilapidated wall.

"It was on the French Riviera."

It was doubtful whether Brenda could have pinpointed the Côte d'Azur on a map, but she had a mental image of an arc of tall palms and an expansive curving bay. Janie had succeeded in conveying an abiding impression.

"They had this marvellous summer together, but it was the year the war broke out and the cousin had to come home suddenly because he had business to attend to."

If Mavis had had any intellectual curiosity, she might have wondered at all the things that Brenda and Janie Goodwin had found to talk about in their brief but apparently intense friendship under a hedge near a sawmill. But Mavis did not ask questions. She did not even reveal whether she was taking any interest in Brenda's story.

"But Miss Goodwin and her old lady weren't in a hurry to come home, though anybody could have told them that there was going to be a war in a few days' time. What happened was that they found their way into Switzerland, and Miss Goodwin got some sort of job, for the Red Cross, or something. I think it was the Red Cross. And the old lady died there, and Miss Goodwin was left on her own. But she had enough money to get by on, and she didn't come home again till the war was over."

They were driving through a small town now, and some of the girls let down the windows and shouted juvenile provocations at a knot of young men sitting astride their massive Japanese motorcycles round a stone market cross.

"Then this cousin went and turned up again. In Switzerland. I don't know what he was supposed to be doing there, and I don't think Miss Goodwin did either. Of course she was over the moon to see him again—but I could tell how it was going to turn out from the way she talked about it."

Now they were entering a motorway from a slip road. The minibus loaded with Technical College students overtook them and there was loud shouting from both parties.

"Of course, she didn't tell me word for word, but it was pretty obvious what had happened. If she had wanted him as badly as she said she did, she shouldn't have let him out of her sight in the first place. She should have come home with him when she had the chance, if you ask me. Like most men," Brenda said, "he wanted it both ways. But Miss Goodwin saw through him in time. She guessed what I'd have known all along—that he must have somebody else at home. What would you do, Mavis, if your boyfriend gave you the big let-down?"

"Dunno," Mavis said. "Never thought about it."

"I know what I'll do, if it ever happens to me."

"What's that, then?"

"I shan't break my heart over it, that's for certain. And I don't think Miss Goodwin did, once she got over the first shock. She said she ought to have known all along that he was no damned good. Even in family matters, they'd never been able to trust him. There were money matters, you see. Something he was supposed to be looking after for Miss Goodwin's brother until he came of age. Some sort of fiddle—I didn't understand it, and Miss Goodwin said that she didn't, either. I think the only ones who did were those who were in the middle of it, and one was as bad as the other, if all the truth were told. She had a terrible childhood, and that's why she always goes about in those funny clothes."

If Mavis had really been interested, she must surely have asked a question about the *sequitur* of that. But she said nothing.

"And something I thought was pathetic: when they brought me back to the Centre, she got out of the car and danced about the hummocks as if she thought she was a kid again. Well, she came home to England, and she came to live at Hempshaw End, and she got married, and that was another thing. That was another big mistake. Some women never learn, do they?" the young oracle asked. "She made a mistake inside a mistake— that's the way she put it. I think there are going to be some big changes in Hempshaw End when all this has blown over. It all happened, you see, because this cousin wrote to her wanting to come here and see her. He had written to her two or three times over the years, but she had always ignored him, just as you or I would have done. But this time she didn't, because one of her sisters had sent her some news about their brother, who had been out of the country for years, but had come back because there was something he had to settle. And Miss Goodwin said, well, he wasn't the only one who had something to settle. That wasn't really hide-and-seek they were playing about the countryside, you know, the morning they had us out looking for a dead body. What was going on was that the brother and the cousin were neither of them very far away—Miss Goodwin had fixed that. But they had to be kept apart until it was the right moment for them to be brought together. And what happened after that I don't

know, because I got stuck upstairs with that bloody
teacher. What do *you* think happened, Mavis?"

"Dunno. It's so boring, innit?"

"It's time we got an interim report on paper," Grimshaw
said. "There are going to be County Councillors asking
to be genned up. Have a bash at it, will you, Beamish?
Good exercise for you. I'll be interested to see how you
tackle it."

Beamish was in the middle of this piece of arduous
composition when the phone rang for him. The message bristled through the CID room like a wind of
change in a cornfield.

"Detective-Sergeant Beamish: a call from Kenya."

Beamish sat with ballpoint poised, and actually succeeded in getting the beginnings of two sentences on
paper.

"I've been a bit worried, Beamish. I don't like travelling all this way and leaving things behind me half-
finished."

"Yes, well—"

"I keep thinking of those cabbage plants I got for
Ernie Walton. They weren't up to much, were they?
But by the time I realized that, it was too late for me to
do anything about it. Be a good lad and get hold of
another thirty, and put them in for him. And there's
another thing—"

"What?"

"I owe Ernie forty quid. Price of paying off a lorry-
driver and a taxi to take Emma Rawlings off for a day
with her grandniece. Get the money back off her, will
you, and let Ernie have it. I'd count it as very good
Neighbouring, if you would. This call's costing the earth,
so I'll ring off now."

"Mr. Mosley—while you're still on the line—"

But Mosley had already cleared the line—without
giving a clue as to how he could be contacted again.

*   *   *

The moment Detective-Superintendent Grimshaw was out of the house, Georgina Crane was in Elizabeth Stirrup's bedroom.

"What did you tell him? Did you hold firm?"

"I told him what you told me to tell him—not a word more."

If Elizabeth Stirrup had managed to appear in command of herself while Grimshaw was questioning her, she flagged the moment the pressure was off.

"Are you quite sure? Grimshaw's no fool—not all the time, anyway."

It had started while Elizabeth was wallowing in her woes after the Daimler had deposited her back at the schoolhouse. Georgina had suddenly burst out in a mood in which Elizabeth had only once seen her before.

At school, Miss Crane had been much liked for the simple reason that she always behaved as if she had respect for even the least effectual of her pupils. Only once had anyone in Elizabeth's generation seen her lose her temper, and that was over some girl who had tried to lie to her without elementary respect for her intelligence.

She had lost her temper again with Elizabeth Stirrup in the early hours of this morning: really lost it—a frightening fury. Elizabeth had said something again about getting away from here as soon as she could without making a nuisance of herself. There was a smarminess about her humility that was the last straw with the older teacher.

"Stop snivelling! Stop feeling sorry for yourself! Stop being so disgustingly self-indulgent! Any woman with blood in her veins would have enjoyed the experience you've just had."

"Enjoyed it!"

"Because you've just had the privilege of looking into somebody else's world—and you've come out of it unscratched."

"They're welcome to their world."

"It's a damned sight better world than any you've set foot in in your life before. And it's taught you nothing, has it?"

"It's taught me that the people up here—"

"Are beneath your contempt? If that's the case, then your contempt isn't worth the curl of your upper lip. These people live their own lives, they fight out their own quarrels—and dispense their own justice. And nothing has done you any harm. All right: a man in a camel-hair coat drove you away against your will."

When the black vintage saloon had deposited Elizabeth back at the gate, Georgina had had no difficulty in bullying the whole truth out of her. It was true, as she had told Grimshaw, that she had left the house with the intention of getting a car to Bradburn from the garage. And she had indeed run into the man in the coat. But he had seen her looking at him too keenly, too curiously, too photographically. She did not know whether it was a real or a pretend gun that he had stuck into her ribs—but he had had to take her off with him for the sake of his own security.

"For the same reason as the Shuttleworth child was taken. Because if she had gone back to her class mates, she could have given Janie Goodwin's position away within minutes."

"So you expect me to support the law-breakers—to compound a felony?"

"Don't be so mealy-mouthed about the law. There are felonies that aren't in the statute book—crimes that a man gets away with without fear of prison gates. And I believe that's the sort of offence that has been rectified within the last twelve hours not many miles from here."

Now that they were alone together, Georgina's anger had subsided, and Elizabeth was like hand-softened modelling-clay in her hands.

"But what if they start questioning me again? What if they try all the interrogators' tricks on me? I know I'd never be able to stand up to it. They'd have me altering my previous statement—and then there are all sorts of things I could be in trouble for."

"Well—start thinking about somebody else's troubles for a change. Elizabeth—what *do* you know? What did you overhear while you were at Barker's Clough?"

"Nothing that I understood. Only that I was among ruthless people."

"You don't begin to know them, Elizabeth."

"The two men were dreadful. The one who took me away—I've no complaint against his behaviour in the car. He was a smoothie. I dare say some women might even have been impressed by him. But the enmity between him and the other—it must have been going on for years."

"I'm quite sure that it has. I think it practically goes back to original sin."

"I thought for a moment that it was going to be a fight to the death. It would have been, but for the others. There was a whole pack of them who came, you know—all local people, I think: and Miss Goodwin was very much in control. Then they suddenly seemed to remember Brenda and me, and hustled us upstairs. And after that I only know what I was able to put together from voices that came up through the floor-boards."

"And what did you make of what you did hear?"

"It was almost like a sort of court. That detective Mosley drove up in the middle of it, but he only peeped in through a window, and then drove off again."

"Wise man! I can only assume that he had helped them to convene this meeting—and then had the sense to play no further active part in it."

"He sets out to be everything in this valley, does he?"

"This valley could be a good deal worse off than it is."

"But it was such a mischief. Just think of the trouble that woman has caused by making it look as if her home had been wrecked."

"I dare say we shall eventually learn—unofficially—all that was behind it."

"Then there was that horrible man who came up in a lorry and started talking about a gallows. I thought there was going to be a lynching."

"Yes—and I dare say you weren't the only one who thought that. I should imagine Janie Goodwin's brother thought so too: he was meant to. I think perhaps we had better get you away from here some time this morning. I've no desire to turn you into a criminal, Elizabeth—but I'd hate you to break under questioning. You might help to identify people who deserve not to be identified. Is there anywhere where you could go and stay?"

"There's a quiet little seaside hotel I sometimes use."

"I think you'd better go there till term begins again. We can't have you used as evidence against John Mosley."

Beamish decided to wait until first dark before planting Ernie Walton's second batch of cabbages. Case-hardened extrovert though he might seem to officers above and below him, there were hidden depths of diffidence about Beamish when it came to certain kinds of public performance. He had no wish to give a second-house demonstration of his horticultural novitiate to the silently watching allotment-holders who were Ernie's neighbours. Consequently, it was alone by moonlight, with a bicycle lamp propped on a brick at the end of a row, that he bedded out a new and healthier-looking platoon of Webb's Favourites. It would have been a good night for watchers of the skies—an unclouded firmament, with Orion and Cassiopeia clearly identifiable by amateurs. Below him were the wanly lighted rectangular windows of a well-lived-in village. Muffled dialogue drifted over from more than one quarter: family circles of great variation in social aspiration were all watching the same situation comedy.

And Beamish was thinking. His mind, liberated by physical activity to which he was applying a good deal of vigour, had gone as fallow as the patch on his right.

There were aspects of this case that he did not think had been properly gone into. The morning of Janie Goodwin's disappearance, for example—how had she actually got away? How had she come out of her gate into the Hempshaw End main street without alerting the whole of Hempshaw End? How had Mosley been able to get into her garden without drawing attention to himself? Because Mosley had dropped his pipe there, under Janie's window—and Beamish was by now convinced that this could only have been an accident. So why had Mosley gone there at all? It could only be, surely, because he had known what plan Janie had in mind, and had looked in to see if the stage had been laid—if the scene of domestic wreckage had been convincingly deployed.

When could he have done this? It had to have been fairly early that morning—before he had gone up to the Protectorate to mow Cromwell's lawn. Again that crucial question: how had he managed not to be seen? And in a sudden access of inspiration that almost made him drive his dibber through his foot, Beamish thought he saw the answer.

But his train of inductive reasoning was interrupted by the sounds of someone behind him. All his protective senses came to the alert. The night was quiet—but by no means empty. Someone had hens roosting in a ramshackle shed from which there drifted a descant of contented murmuring. Someone else had interlaced his seed beds with hanging strips cut from kitchen foil that rustled in the slight air-movement. But the new element was of a distinctly human approach—that of a man who was taking no particular care to conceal his presence. Beamish waited until the newcomer was directly behind him, then swung round with his dibber at the on-guard position.

"Nay, lad—tha's no call to attack me."

Ernie Walton. There was enough light from the bicycle lamp for him to see the results of Beamish's activity. Ernie was not given to open statements of gratitude—but, at least, he did not seem able to find anything to criticize here.

"Aye," he said, coming as near as ever in his life to expressing appreciation. "Did you get to see Mr. Mosley, then?"

"Actually, no. I'd half a mind to slip off to Africa for half an hour this morning, but it was standing-room only, so I didn't fancy the trip."

Ernie was silent for a short time. Sarcasm puzzled him: he saw no call for it.

"But he's been in touch with me, and I've got forty quid for you in my pocket."

They walked back down to the village together, and Beamish counted out the money under a wheezing streetlamp.

"Aye—he's a good lad, is Mosley."

As he stuffed the roll of notes into the back pocket of his trousers, Walton seemed to be oozing unaccustomed good will.

"He put some time in on this business, you know."

"I'm sure he did."

"I mean, but for Mosley, we'd never have got together like that."

"No?"

"Who'd have ever known who they all were?"

"Who indeed?"

"When Goodwin went broke, you know, it was hard on this valley. He paid half a crown in the pound, when everything was settled. That's not a lot."

"I can see that."

"It may be all right for these big London firms. They can juggle their books. But when it's three years' milk, and a couple of years' eggs—I've known Wilson Goodwin, you know, come round to pay two quid on account—

and go off with another fiver's worth of stuff in the back of his car. It comes hard on poor folk, Mr. Beamish."

"I'm sure it does."

"Janie was determined we should all be paid back in full—even if it went thirty years before that brother of hers showed up again. And she said it wasn't to be done through the courts. Because that way there'd be preferential creditors and God knows what to be considered— and it would go another five years. But she'd no idea who was owed what. So she set Mosley on finding out and getting us all together. He's a bloody good detective, is Mosley."

There was another call that Beamish made on impulse, and that was on the Sisters Ledman. It came into his mind because of what he had unexpectedly learned from Ernie. He knew that Lois and Laetitia had not told him all they knew. They had probably even included a few downright lies, if only because their life's training had been to keep all knowledge to themselves whenever possible.

It was after ten at night, but there was light behind the Ledmans' downstairs window as he drove past on his way home from Ernie's. He pulled up outside their gate and tapped with their knocker. At least, he tried to tap, but the heavy brasswork with its cat-and-fiddle insignia echoed sepulchrally from one side of the village to the other.

There seemed to be something going on inside the house, as if special preparations had to be made before the front door could be opened. When it did open, a chin was thrust out just above the chain, but they both seemed wholly delighted to see him, and positively hustled him into their over-heated living-room.

Their home computer stood on the table, among a tangle of plugs and cables. But it was not their domestic accounts, nor a schedule of their wide-ranging penny-share portfolio that was on display. It was an intergalactic invasion by creatures who looked like a cross between bats and flying bulls.

"You must excuse us, Mr. Beamish—just the last half-hour of the day, you know."

"You must excuse me, too, ladies. But I happened to be passing and I just wondered . . ."

He wondered whether they would produce the ginger wine. But hospitality did not seem to be in their minds tonight. Perhaps they suspected that he was only here for the tipple.

"I just wondered whether you'd thought of anything else that you felt I ought to know."

"Oh, I don't think so, Mr. Beamish," Laetitia said.

"What sort of thing was it you had in mind?" Lois asked.

He noticed that even as she spoke, the little one's eyes strayed involuntarily towards the screen.

"We are really not at all well informed, you know."

"Those other people, with whom you went to the farmhouse at Barker's Clough—how many of them did you actually know?"

"Well—one or two. Mr. Walton. And old Stephen Blamire from Hadley Dale. I must say we were surprised to see him there. It turned out that his father used to supply firewood to the Hall."

Her eyes again wandered towards the star-war. Beamish got up and went to the keyboard.

"How do you fire the cannon?"

"Tap Z or X for left front, N or M for right. A and L for enfilading fire from the flanks."

Beamish pressed a key and one of the bat-bulls exploded in a purple puff.

"Watch out, Sergeant: you'll have a whole file of them coming down through that gap."

It ended up with his challenging the pair of them together. He was no match for their knowledge of the idiosyncrasies of the game—but it broke the ice. It was not long after that the information began to flow. Secretive though they were by both temperament and

training, the Ledman sisters were paradoxically long-
ing to talk.

"Of course, I suppose we were the only couple at
that farm who knew who Harvey Carlyon was."

"Harvey Carlyon?"

Beamish knew that he had to be supremely careful
what questions he put and how he put them. If he drew
attention too sharply to his own ignorance, he might
remind them fatally that they were behaving like trai-
tors. Likewise, it would be better if they more than half
forgot that he had an official capacity. All the same,
there were details on which he knew he might desperately need patient guidance.

"It's a Cornish name," Laetitia Ledman said, and
seemed to think for one exasperating moment that that
information was adequate. But she glanced at her sister
as if asking permission to proceed.

"He was a second cousin of Janie Goodwin's, one
generation back."

"His father was Wilson Goodwin Senior's uncle on
his mother's side."

"We used to know a lot of what was going on, because we used to hear our father tell our mother."

"Our father was a bank clerk, you see."

"They knew a lot of things at the bank."

"There were people who said that old Wilson Goodwin need never have gone bankrupt. They said it was
only a move to put his funds where his creditors could
not get at them."

"He only paid half a crown in the pound."

"Some of his holdings were in his wife's name. That's
the way it's often done."

"Only you don't have to overdo it."

"And knowing all we do about Jessica Goodwin's
goings-on, we'd never have trusted her with much of
our capital, would we, Lois?"

"Not unless we had her chained to our wrists. So
there had to be an intermediary. That was where Harvey Carlyon came in."

"He was what they call a nominee. He would sign transfer certificates and hand money over when Wilson Goodwin needed it."

"Not the most reliable way of stashing away your treasure," Beamish said.

"Well, of course, Harvey Carlyon must have taken a whacking commission."

"Not only that. It was always believed—they certainly believed it at the bank—that Wilson Goodwin had some sort of hold over his uncle. Something he knew about some transaction or other."

"You mean blackmail?"

"We never heard that word used, did we, Laetitia?"

They both looked grave. In the Middle Ages it had been considered obscene to mouth the word "plague."

"But you can see, Mr. Beamish, that what worked for one generation wouldn't necessarily work with another."

"They had a good laugh in the bank when the whisper went the rounds that Harvey Carlyon had done the dirty on his cousin."

"It was during the war, and young Wilson Goodwin had had to go into the army."

"He did rather well for himself, we believe."

"Young Harvey Carlyon did rather well for *himself*, too, once Wilson Goodwin's back was turned."

"Harvey Carlyon didn't go into the army."

"No. But he was doing war work. He had to keep going abroad."

"He liked people to think it was war work—"

"Now, Lois, be careful what you're saying. Stick to what you know is true."

"He was something to do with economic warfare."

"All kinds of things had to do with economic warfare."

There was now a flush in both women's cheeks. Something was going on between them that Beamish did not understand.

"How can you know all this?" he asked them.

"It was bank talk. The bank was owed money too. Anyway . . ."

Lois took a deep breath and brought her narrative back to what, presumably, she thought she knew was true.

"When Wilson Goodwin was demobilized, he came back to find that the Goodwin capital was a thing of the past. Watch out, Titia—the Sergeant's hand is hovering near the enfilading key."

Beamish had taken over the role of invader now, with the wits of the women jointly pitted against him. He lost a whole rank of his flying bulls to flanking fire, much to their exuberant satisfaction.

"So Wilson Goodwin had to make do for himself."

"He went to South America."

"As a planter."

"Growing coffee."

"Well. There are two opinions about that."

"Just remember that Mr. Beamish is a policeman, Lois."

"Some say there's only one cash crop worth growing where Wilson Goodwin's been farming."

"Lois!"

Laetitia even let her concentration on the electronic game lapse while she impressed a point on Beamish.

"You must not take too much notice of my sister, Mr. Beamish. She watches too much lurid television. We haven't heard of Wilson Goodwin for years. We think that perhaps he has come back to England because of the latest big arrest of drug-pushers; but that is pure speculation on our part. We think he may have come back to organize a new sales network. I'm afraid we are not always as jealous of our neighbours' reputations as the Good Book would have us be—but that is only when we are talking between ourselves."

"Quite!" Beamish said, hoping to bring back the conversation to discipline by a firm but friendly tone. Lois's hand shot out unexpectedly, and one of his vanguard bulls exploded.

"Your mind's not on the game, Mr. Beamish."

"There is one thing that intrigues me," Beamish said. "Though I dare say you are as puzzled by it as I am."

"Oh, we are puzzled by any number of things, Mr. Beamish."

For a few seconds it looked as if their curiosity was going to get the better of their sportswomanship, but Lois's hand suddenly stabbed at the keyboard.

"How did Janie Goodwin contrive to get these two men up here?"

"Ah! I'm afraid you have us there, Sergeant."

"I'm assuming that Harvey Carlyon is the one who was seen about in an opulent overcoat. But I have not heard of any public sightings of Wilson Goodwin."

"He was certainly there. And you should have seen their faces when they recognized each other. No, I'm afraid we've been beating our brains in vain about how she brought it off."

"But we do have our theories," the other said.

He had to listen to them all—and outlandish was the word for them. Janie had appealed to Harvey Carlyon in the name of her undying love. Or perhaps she had offered to sell him some letters that he had written to her when she had first started travelling abroad in the 1930s. The sisters Ledman clearly read widely in the realms of popular naughtiness. They were less fluent in their theories about what bait might have been held out to Wilson Goodwin. Perhaps his sister had offered him contacts about a shady land-deal in a tract of shooting-moor that nobody used any more. Or maybe she had suggested growing marijuana in some secret corner of Upper Calesdale. Or perhaps he might extend his markets to the young people at the Field Studies Centre. In this seam the ingenuity of the Ledmans was wearing thin. Beamish moved them on to a fresh angle.

"But when she had finally got you all together at Barker's Clough—how did she get her brother to agree so readily to settle his debts?"

"Ah, well—"

"It was overfacing for them, you know—even for two experienced men like that."

"They did not know what was happening to them. Here they were, ushered into this roomful of people, some of them looking pretty ugly."

"Even we were wondering what lengths Janie Goodwin was prepared to go to."

"Janie was very powerful. Very powerful indeed."

"Though her two sisters didn't help much."

"They were too civilized."

"Altogether too civilized," Laetitia said.

Tall, gaunt and dogmatic, one's first impression of Laetitia was of undying latterday puritan. What was there about her that made it unsurprising that she should condemn "civilization" in another woman? Was this the sort of thing that was meant—the phrase came unbidden into Beamish's mind—when men used the expression "Mosley's people?"

"But even in spite of them, the atmosphere was pretty electric."

"I know *I* was scared out of my wits."

"It was peculiar, really, because I wouldn't have said we were a particularly scary bunch."

"Yet I could see that both Mr. Goodwin and Mr. Carlyon kept looking at us furtively."

"Even at us two, Mr. Beamish. Several times I felt their eyes resting on me."

"Fancy anyone being afraid of a couple like us!"

They both giggled.

"Mind you, I think they truly believed they were going to be hanged. I suppose that makes some difference to a man's attitude."

"They believed they were going to be hanged? You mean that she threatened them in so many words?"

"Not in so many words. But hanging was very much in the air."

"All she actually said was, 'By the way, the execution shed's just across the yard.' "

"And then that man came up with the lorry."

"Now there was a character for you."

"He looked just like a public hangman."

"Titia—how can you possibly know what a public hangman looks like?"

"Well—he talked like one. 'Right,' he said. 'Who's for the nine o'clock walk? Who am I operating on this morning, ma'am?' "

" 'There are two of them,' she said, and you could see they couldn't be sure whether she was fooling or not."

Beamish got very little else out of the Ledmans. He gathered that the showdown in Emma Rawlings's farmhouse had been a *tour de force* of atmosphere and personality. Janie Goodwin must have effected something akin to mass hypnosis. And the Misses Ledman had been as captivated as anyone present.

It was a relief to come away from their house, to drive up and over the darkened moors. There was one more task that Beamish felt he ought to do before he went to bed. While working on the allotment, he had suddenly thought of a way in which Janie Goodwin could have got out of her cottage without being seen on the Friday morning. He thought it worth an *ad hoc* memo to Grimshaw.

Sir: We were wondering why the population of Hempshaw End did not see Mrs. Cromwell come away from her place on Friday morning—and how Inspector Mosley managed to visit the house unobserved. I think I have hit upon the answer: perhaps Hempshaw End was watching something else at the time.

I propose to make efforts to discover what.

18

As Grimshaw came away from his talk with the Cromwells, it looked at first as if Hempshaw End was on its way to church; except that the population was moving in ones, twos and family groups in the opposite direction from St. Stephen's spire. A vicar with modern views on PR might have accompanied his flock towards the mock execution.

Grimshaw had mixed feelings about attending. But he was under no doubt as to where his duty lay. The dispatch of Dr. Crippen was to be re-enacted in a shed at the back of Sarah Bramwell's cottage, and he was already within sight of it when he noticed that some people—definitely a minority—were detaching themselves from the main axis of advance. A thin line was straggling towards the exit from the village where Georgina Crane's schoolhouse lay. His first thought was that this was perhaps a deputation calling on her in protest against this morning's sadism; obviously she must be a repository for any village problem to which there was apparently no answer.

But this lesser crowd continued on up past the school. When they reached the bridge across the Old Railway, they climbed the wall and let themselves down the embankment towards a plate-layer's hut by whose door a man and a woman were collecting money.

That was how Detective-Superintendent Grimshaw came to attend Hempshaw End's rival hanging. It was a

very amateurish ceremony—badly conceived, badly
staged and badly acted. It was not helped by the fact
that there was insufficient room inside the hut for such
a spectacle, and if the organizer had not moved the
spectators back at the critical moment, at least half a
dozen of them would have disappeared into the pit
when the trap was sprung.

The effigy was of sacking stuffed with straw, and it
was not heavy enough to tauten the rope convincingly
as it fell. Its facial features were an elementary daub not
meant to represent anyone in particular, but its clothing was an obvious pastiche of Janie Goodwin's.

A cheer went up when the body slithered off the
boards. It was in a good cause: the takings were ear-
marked for next year's "Blue Peter" charity, whatever
that might be.

Georgina Crane did not call on Janie Cromwell until a
mature hour of the Monday morning. She found Janie
hard at work, clearly using the reorganization of her
furniture as an excuse for a more fundamental spring-
cleaning than she had undertaken for some years. Not
that Janie ever allowed her home to be grubby; there
was simply too much in it.

Georgina picked up a small pot that contained a
sad-looking specimen of *Opuntia versicolor*.

"Doesn't this need potting up?"

"On the contrary, I've only just potted it down. Sometimes these things prefer their roots held tight, you
know."

Janie was wearing a plastic apron decorated with a
poster design for a well-known brand of Worcester
sauce. Georgina noticed that under it she was wearing
more modern clothes than she usually paraded—not
contemporary, by a long chalk—rather in the "Granny"
style of a few years ago, which had been some women's
counter to the mini-skirt.

"So, Janie—you seem to have pulled it off."

"There were times when I didn't think I was going to. And if you hadn't spotted that piece in the paper about Wilson coming home—"

"I didn't know when I showed it you just what I was setting in motion."

"I didn't really believe I'd ever succeed in getting my brother up here."

"I wish you'd tell me how you managed it."

"Old Emma Rawlings's farm: I had it passed to him along the vine that that was just another way in which my father had shunted some of his assets into safe keeping. The Rawlingses have always been so scrupulously honest. They'd run the place for years on my father's behalf. There was an accumulation of profits in the bank, and old Emma Rawlings was worried stiff what she ought to do with them."

"Is there a word of truth in that story?"

"None whatever."

"That place at Barker's Clough hasn't been farmed for years; not since Rawlings died."

"Wilson was not to know that. In any case, I added a few frills. Like that the deeds are worth a mint of money because of the new link that's going to join the two motorways."

"And your brother fell for all that?"

"He wouldn't have done if he'd heard it from my lips. He'd have smelled a rat straight away. But I fed it to him through a pair of my sisters. They're so bored stiff with the lives that they lead, they'll grab hold of anything that has a touch of spice about it."

"But what about your cousin? How did you get him here?"

"Same story—only he seems to have got hold of the idea that this was another Goodwin holding that ought to have been in his keeping. Funny how some people seem always to get hold of the wrong end of the stick."

"Especially when they're encouraged to."

Janie had an old-fashioned whistling kettle. It chose

this moment to call her into the kitchen. She went and made coffee.

"It was a queer feeling, seeing Harvey again. It surprised me that I no longer hated him. It also surprised me that I could ever have had any other feeling for him."

"But your brother and your cousin didn't come to blows?"

"Oh, good heavens, no—that's not the sort of men they are. They hate each other like poison—but neither's going to gaol to get even with the other. They are *businessmen*, Miss Crane."

"Janie—why did you have to go to such lengths? Couldn't you just have wandered off and met them somewhere? Why all the melodrama?"

"Noll Cromwell," Janie said, packing volumes of meaning into three syllables. "He had to believe that I was beyond his help—otherwise he'd have been there helping. And I didn't want that: it could have been fatal. If he had known which two men I was meeting, he wouldn't have been able to contain himself. Noll's subtle way of dealing with that sort of tricky situation would have been to issue a few thick ears."

Janie looked knowingly at Georgina. An outside observer might have concluded that they had known each other very well over a very long period.

"Besides, I thought it would be no bad idea to have the hills swarming with constabulary. There could have been accidents, and help might have come in useful. It did not occur to me that it was schoolkids the hills were going to swarm with."

"You didn't find it too difficult dodging the cordon?"

"No—as I told that child that I had to impound—I moved on the extreme flank of the party until they were clear of my danger zone."

"I still don't know how you managed to get out of your cottage in the first place without being spotted by half the village."

"Because the village wasn't looking. It was easy. I

know a lorry-driver who likes being a bit of a clown. You know that gallowses have become a hot property in the Hemp Valley of late? Well, there's an optimistic consortium in the village who are trying to cash in on it in a big way. They fancy themselves as entrepreneurs—but they haven't much in the way of resources. They have no storage space and no business premises, so, having bought the thing, they decided to store it in the old plate-layer's hut, where they could also demonstrate it to potential customers. It was transported there on Friday morning—so I persuaded my friend to carry it up on the back of his wagon, all set up for action—and with a body dressed up in my clothes all strapped, noosed and ready for its penitential journey. It drove out of the village by the back way—so you can imagine what everybody was looking at. All I had to do was walk out through my gate. The street was deserted."

"But didn't the search-party visit the hut?"

"They did—at least, Sam Kettle's wife did. Sam's one of the consortium, so she made sure she was one of the squad that went up the Railway. Someone actually shouted to her over a wall, asking what she'd found in there. 'Only a couple of beer cans, rolling about on the floor,' she told them."

Janie replenished Georgina's cup.

"You're playing this in a very low key, Janie. On the quiet, you're a bit of a miracle-worker, aren't you? The only help you had was a geriatric bunch of creditors and creditors' relicts."

"And my lorry-driver." Janie grinned. "And don't underestimate that posse of mine. They looked like a crowdscene from one of Hell Bruegel's more sinister visions. I'd told Wilson and Harvey that they were in the mood for a lynching: just made it sound like a silly joke at first, you know. Oh, and I'd warned them that there were going to be two women present who knew a great deal about the old days, and were thinking of having their memoirs ghost-written. The Misses Ledman: I felt sorry for the dirty looks they kept getting. But it

was my lorry-driver who tipped the balance. A ca-
daverous-looking man—he happened to come by to
collect the gallows that Emma Rawlings had sold to a
Holiday Camp at Filey."

"Happened to come by—"

"And he had a wonderful line of patter, Miss Crane.
You could see those two men beginning to wonder what
was a joke and what wasn't. And there were a lot of
people in that room—jamming it up—blocking all the
ways out—"

"And a chairperson who knew just how to galvanize
the company."

But Janie made light of that.

"My brother Wilson paid out enough money to give a
lot of local pleasure—perhaps even to alleviate a little
hardship here and there. And the sum total of it was
something that Wilson Goodwin will hardly miss. I
could see when we got his nerves to the state when
he'd have shelled out to reduce his stay in that house
by half an hour."

"But how did he pay out? Cheques wouldn't be much
use to most of those people."

"I was carrying cash. The cheque was made out to
me. It won't bounce. Wilson knows I would stop at
nothing."

"And what now, Janie?"

While they had been talking, Georgina had been
looking attentively round the room. Janie was doing her
housework to a system—and it was not the system of a
woman who was simply flicking a duster and wielding a
polishing-cloth. It looked more like the activity of one
who was doing some large-scale sorting out of possessions—as if she were contemplating moving house.

"What now? I'm not quite in a position to tell you
that yet, Miss Crane."

"You mean it takes two?"

"I mean I sometimes feel like that poor little cactus
over there. I need potting down. My roots have had too
much space for too long."

She smiled. Janie had a very informative smile—when she felt in an informative mood.

"Do you know why we never lived together, Noll and I, Miss Crane? Do you know what we fell out about, on our way home from church? All I happened to say was how many spoonfuls of sugar I thought it healthy for a man to have in his tea. And all Noll said was that he hoped I hadn't brought my fish knives and forks. That was enough for both of us; we recognized something. This was the moment we'd both been living for—when we were going to start changing each other's habits. And that was something neither of us would stand for. But maybe we're wise enough now to run the risks."

The Assistant Chief Constable handed back to Detective-Superintendent Grimshaw the definitive report that Sergeant Beamish had written.

"He has quite a good classifying mind, this young man."

"Yes. I believe he could go quite a long way—if only—"

"Quite."

The ACC sat back in his chair. "When do we expect Mosley back?"

"The end of next week, sir."

"There is nothing in Sergeant Beamish's admirable summary that implicates Mosley in any way. In fact, Mosley is not mentioned."

"As you remember, sir, Mosley has been on leave throughout the operative period."

The Assistant Chief Constable asked for the report back and affixed at the top and bottom of it a rubber stamp which he reached for without having to look what he was doing.

NO ACTION.

* * *

An extended family of squatters was moving out of the
new stone house that had been built on the outskirts of
Hempshaw End some years ago. Half of them were
going to live in The Protectorate, the others in a small
cottage in the heart of the village. Sounds suggestive of
domestic commotion were carried across the roofs and
copses on the evening on which Janie and Noll moved
in together. For some minutes there appeared to be an
interchange of kitchen utensils, and then an impact
suggesting that a flying flat-iron had made contact
with a pane of glass. But the occupants were still in
residence the next morning, and appeared to be flour-
ishing.

ABOUT THE AUTHOR

"JOHN GREENWOOD" is the pseudonym of a British crime writer who has published numerous mysteries under his own name. Of him, *The New York Times Book Review* says, "Whoever he is . . . he has a deft hand and a knowledge of small-town people. He makes Inspector Mosley a very real human being." The author lives and works in Norwich, England.